The Man Who Hated Television

and other stories

ALSO BY JULIAN SYMONS

JULIAN SYMONS

The Man Who Hated Television

and other stories

MACMILLAN

First published 1995 by Macmillan London

an imprint of Macmillan General Books
Cavaye Place London SW10 9PG
and Basingstoke

Associated companies throughout the world

ISBN 0 333 63230 3

A CIP catalogue record for this book is available from
the British Library

Typeset by CentraCet Limited, Cambridge
Printed by Mackays of Chatham PLC, Chatham, Kent

Contents

The Man Who
Hated Television

You say it may help if I tell the story of my father's tragedy as I saw it, and I will try to do that. The origin of it was that my father, Jacob Pryde, hated television.

There was a reason for this. His own father was an insurance salesman who cheated his employers by claiming commission on non-existent sales which he justified by forged orders and invoices. When this could not be covered up any longer, he took his wife out in their car, stopped in a quiet country road, and shot first her and then himself.

My father was small, I believe five years old. He was taken away from home by an aunt, and told his parents had gone on holiday. He learned of their deaths because he was watching the TV news when an item was shown with pictures of the car and their bodies. I'm told that for some time after that he screamed whenever the television was switched on. So it is not surprising that he refused to have a set in our home.

Television was not the only thing father hated. I think he also hated his wife Susan, and perhaps he hated the people to whom he sold the rare books in which he dealt, books he sometimes said he would sooner have kept on his own shelves in the extension added to our little house in Wandsworth, which is a district in south-west London. The extension was called the library, but really it was just a

1

brick addition to the house, joined to it by a covered passageway.

So did my father hate everybody? Not quite. He loved one person, his daughter, Elvira. Me.

These were the characters in the tragedy, one that seems to me in retrospect inevitable. There was also Doctor Finale, but of course he did not exist. Let me tell the story.

There was a time – the pictures in my mind flicker uncertainly like those in an old film – when father was a lover, not a hater. I remember, or *think* I remember for it is hard to be sure about such scenes from early years, a time when father was happy, and loving not only to me but also to Susan. I see him bending over my cot, lifting me out, his moustache tickling my neck so that I scream with laughter, and he laughs too. I see him holding my mother, they are performing a kind of dance across the room, then they collapse on to a bed, I am standing up in my cot watching, she shrieks something, he cries out, and I cry out too because I think he is hurting her. Later they hold me, pass me from one to the other, make cooing, encouraging sounds.

There are other pictures, similarly fuzzy, particularly of Susan in the kitchen. She loved the kitchen, and was a great cook. I see her busy with a fruit cake, making pancakes on Shrove Tuesday and throwing them up and catching them in the pan, putting a joint of beef in the oven. She is always cheerful, often laughing. Sometimes she sang, out of tune, a snatch of a popular song. Father was in the extension or library, cataloguing his old dark books, cleaning them, perhaps even reading them. She would send me in to tell him when a meal was ready.

I remember the day when her laughter stopped. I was very young, four or five, but I remember it.

She was cooking something, I don't know what, something in a pan with hot fat. I was playing beside the kitchen table near her, perhaps putting a doll to bed, I can't remember. She was singing. Then suddenly her song changed to a scream. I saw there were flames in the pan, bright yellow, and some fat had splashed on to her hand. My father ran in from the extension. His first thought was for me, that I might be splashed by the burning fat. He picked me up, and as he did so he or I must have knocked against the pan. The fat in it went straight into my mother's face. Then there were screams and screams.

When she came out of hospital after the skin grafts one side of her face was stiff and unreal as if it was made of wood or hard wax, and the left side of her mouth was fixed in what looked like a sneering grin. When I first saw her I cried, ran away and hid.

From that time our life changed. My father could not bear ugly things. Susan was ugly now, and I think he blamed her for it. He spoke to her as little as possible, and would sometimes ask if she couldn't look at him without that grin on her face. She had changed too. She was very silent now, never sang, looked after the house as before, and cooked, but took no pleasure in it. She rarely left the house, never with him. I don't think he offered to take her.

His attention now was focused almost exclusively on me. We spent hours together in the library where he told me about the books, which were valuable and why, showed me how to distinguish between typefaces and tell which was appropriate for a particular kind of book or size of page, the way in which he described books when he sent out lists to attract the interest of possible clients.

The whole of his business was carried on through these lists or catalogues, which he prepared with immense care. When he received an order he would be both pleased and upset, upset because he hated to part with any of the books. Orders would be packed first in tissue paper, then plastic wrapping, cardboard, and finally thick brown paper. He tried vainly to teach me what he called the art of packing. In part this was because my fingers seemed all thumbs when I tried to put the wrapping round, but also I felt that to take such care about packing a book was ridiculous. Not until I was thirteen or fourteen did I realize that all those evenings and weekends spent in the library were preparation for the time when he expected me to carry on the business. One day he showed me a sheet of the writing paper headed *Jacob Pryde, Fine Books*, and said: 'The time will come when this will be *Jacob and Elvira Pryde*, and then just *Elvira*.'

I knew then that this would not be so. I had little interest in books, none in bookselling. Those hours spent in the library or extension were time wasted for me, hours of boredom. Why did I not say so? Because I both admired and feared my father. He was a handsome man, rather above the ordinary height, slim, hair and moustache iron-grey, face lean, nose aquiline, expression generally stern.

He had only two recreations in life apart from his books. One was his car, an old Mercedes which he cared for as if it were a child, washing, leathering and polishing it weekly. The other was a local club for those who, like him, had been in the Territorial Army. He had somehow managed to retain the revolver used by his own father, and he used it to practise in the club's little shooting gallery. He took me to the club once, but I did not care for the beer-drinking back-slapping atmosphere, and perhaps he realized this. Certainly he never suggested I should pay another visit.

And my mother, she who had laughed and sung? She was like a lamed bird, trying always to hide the damaged part of her face with its unintended sneer. Are you thinking I should have pitied her, loved her? No doubt I ought to have done, but in truth her appearance repelled me and I took no pains to conceal the fact. Of course she noticed my behaviour, and it must have hurt her.

This may sound like a miserable household, yet when young one becomes accustomed to any way of life. What I missed most was a television set. At school all the girls talked about the programmes, the sexy women and the hunky men ('hunky' was a great word at the time among my friends – 'He's really hunky' meant more than sexy, rather like 'macho' but intelligent and understanding as well). I hadn't seen the hunky men on TV, couldn't talk about them. I felt deprived, and illogically blamed my mother, and not my father.

At fourteen I began smoking pot and using amphetamines. I also had my first sexual coupling, with a boy who acted with me in the school play. These were experiments, I found them pleasant and continued experimenting. The boys were callow, not hunky, the drugs soothing rather than exciting. I know psychiatrists attribute what they call the early resort to sex and drugs to the nature of my home life. Personally I put it down to being deprived of TV. If I'd seen hunky men on the screen I don't think I'd have started experimenting with a schoolboy.

One day, under the soothing influence of speed (I know it's supposed to excite, but can only say I *felt* perfectly calm), I told Jacob my name would never be on the writing paper. For a moment he seemed not to have heard, then he asked what I meant. He was in the midst of a tedious exposition about the qualities of some rare edition he had recently bought. I picked up the book – though it was not really a book but a pamphlet, something to do with Swinburne or Rossetti or one of that lot – and said I wasn't interested, everything to do with his business bored me. As I spoke the pamphlet drifted away and sank slowly to the floor, yet some of it remained in my hand. I had torn it in two, an act performed quite unconsciously and at the time causing me no alarm. I repeat that speed *felt* soothing.

Jacob – it was at this moment he changed in my perception from *father* to *Jacob* – at first looked unbelievingly from what remained in my hand to the papers on the floor. Then I saw his hand raised, heard the sound as it struck my cheek (the sound, though, faint and fading like an echo). The paper I held was removed from my grasp, and then he was on the floor picking up the rest of the

5

pamphlet, saying something I failed to hear or understand. But I could not mistake the look in his dark eyes as we stood close together, the pages still in his trembling hand. It was a look of hatred.

I ran out of the library, my feet seeming to bounce lightly on the ground, and spent the rest of the evening in my room. It had been my custom to kiss Jacob's cheek, and that of my mother – the good side of course – when I came down to breakfast, but on the next morning my lips brushed only her cheek. Then I sat down. Jacob stared at me. I stared back. Then he spoke, not to me nor to Susan, simply a ruler laying down the law in his kingdom.

'Elvira has been stupidly disobedient. She has destroyed a valuable first edition. She says also that she does not wish to do the work for which I have trained her, as my assistant and eventual partner. She must be taught obedience. Elvira will receive no allowance for a month, nor leave this house in the evening without my permission. Her evenings will be spent with me in the library, learning more about her future occupation.'

But, you will say, how could anybody talk like that? This was the twentieth century, the place London and not some rural area where time had stood still. I was fifteen years old. I can only say that strange things happen in the heart of great cities, and that Jacob Pryde was an unusual, an extraordinary man. The fixity of his dark gaze was compelling, it excluded any possibility of doubt that he would be obeyed. He drove me to school that day in the Mercedes, sitting bolt upright, immovable as a statue. When we arrived he said he would be waiting for me in the afternoon. I saw the future stretching before me, as it seemed endlessly, long days in the classrooms and longer evenings in the library forced to learn more about the world of book dealing I had come to detest. That evening my mother, the wounded bird, said in a moment when we were alone that she was sorry, there was nothing she could do. I knew this was true. Jacob had bent her to his will, as he now meant to bend me.

Yet this *was* the twentieth century, I *was* fifteen years old and not literally a prisoner. There were people I knew through the drugs circuit, and through the school play I had met one or two students at RADA. On the third night spent under Jacob's Law I took money from my mother's purse, left a note in my bedroom saying I was not coming back but would be in touch, and shinned down a drainpipe outside my bedroom window. I spent that night on the sofa of a girl at RADA.

I don't want to describe the next six years in detail. I slept around (contracting neither AIDS nor any venereal disease), worked in shops, got hooked on drugs and then unhooked myself when I realized what they were doing to me – and I made a career in TV. I had hated those old smelly books Jacob caressed with such pleasure, and was bored by the theatre, yet I wanted some sort of career connected with the arts, modern arts, and what is more modern than TV? It's here today and forgotten next week, and I like that too. I hate the sort of stuff Jacob loved, that lingers on and on, stuff people like simply because it's old.

Anyway, I made a career on the box, first with the help of the RADA student, who introduced me to her agent. I'm supposed to have a wistful little-girl-lost look, and I played mostly what you might call victim parts in sitcoms and thrillers, never a lead player. I suppose I was typecast, but typecasting can have its advantages. If you're lucky it can keep you in steady work. And I was lucky. At twenty-one I had my own little flat, a bit of money in the bank, no steady boyfriend.

I used my own name, Elvira Pryde, why not? I talked quite often to Susan on the phone, but Jacob would never speak. Soon after I started appearing on the box I paid for a set and had it sent to her. Of course I knew Jacob would never buy her one, but I couldn't have imagined his reaction. When I rang to ask if she had enjoyed seeing me, she told me Jacob had been angry when he saw the set, and had been beside himself when he heard it came from me. He made her look while he smashed it up with a hammer, then threw it away. Perhaps I should have realized then that he was crazy.

Susan told me about this without apparent emotion. The accident had changed not only her face but also her voice, making it dry and thin. I asked why she didn't leave Jacob, come and live with me. She said she was his wife, what would he do without her? I was going to say what I thought of that when she added: 'He's a good man, you know. He only wanted the best for you.'

'The *best*.' I couldn't believe what I heard.

'He loves you. You know that.'

'He's mad. He must be, to hate television the way he does.'

'He wants you to come back. He would make you a partner at once. And I would be pleased.'

She said it in that same dry voice. Suppose she had pleaded with me, would it have made a difference? I don't think so.

Then I got the job as Doctor Finale's assistant. That was a real boost for me, regular work in a thirteen-part series, and a bigger part than anything I'd had. After the tragedy, of course, the show came off the air. It's never mentioned now, and I don't suppose anything like it will be done again. So I'd better describe it briefly.

It was called a horror soap, and that's about right. Doctor Finale, as his name suggests, was a kind of last resort. One man came to him because he was dying of AIDS and believed his heir had deliberately arranged his infection; a woman wanted revenge on the man who'd killed her young daughter in a car accident and been acquitted at trial; a man whose family had been wiped out by a terrorist bomb wanted

Doctor Finale's help in turning himself into a living bomb that would blow up the terrorist state's embassy.

Mostly these were revenge stories, always they were violent. Doctor Finale, whose degree was in psychology and not medicine, had no regard for the law and was absolutely ruthless. Once he discovered a client had been trying to trick him, and arranged a trap that left him financially ruined and physically damaged. Doctor Finale respected only money and power. He was an emotional sadist who treated everybody, clients, opponents and his own assistants, with contempt. Those who did not hate him worshipped him, and I was one of the worshippers. He was played by Lester Morton, a handsome actor in his forties made up to look suitably sinister. I was his secretary Jennifer, a prissy worshipper who was the subject of constant sneers at her accent, love life and lack of clothes sense.

Lester was apologetic. 'I've never played such an A1 bastard,' he said. 'I don't know why you stay with him.'

He laughed, and I did too. 'It's your psychic magnetism, Doctor. That and the viewing figures.' Lester was undeniably an attractive man, everybody said so. And we all knew the show was a success. There had been a short series before I came into it, starting as a cult oddity admired by a few critics. Then it had shot up in the ratings, gaining more viewers every week. One producer, asked to explain its success, said: 'Sadism and violence, how can it fail?' It's always nice to be associated with success, although something about my scenes with Lester made me faintly uneasy.

One day when I rang Susan her voice seemed duller and drier than usual. I asked her if something was wrong.

'This play you are in . . .'

'Not really a play, it's a series. About someone called Doctor Finale, and people who come to him with problems.'

'This Doctor Finale, what is he like?'

'He's a monster.'

'But what does he look like?' Before I could reply she went on: 'Does he look like your father?'

The question stunned me. Lester was balding a little and wore a grey wig, he was made up round the eyes and had a way of opening them wide and then half-closing them that was frightening, his complexion was dark and his nose aquiline – was it a likeness to Jacob that had made me feel uneasy when playing scenes with him? My mother went on to say that at one of the book sales Jacob attended, somebody had congratulated him on my success as a TV actress. That would have been sufficiently uncongenial to him, but the man continued, saying that the principal actor had been made up to look exactly like Jacob. He added that other dealers had noticed it and it had caused much amusement.

Susan was upset. She said Jacob thought I had deliberately arranged that the actor should look like him, that I was sneering at him by making an odious character recognizable as Jacob. I tried to make her understand how absurd it was to suppose an unimportant actress like me could have had any part in the casting.

'This actor who is playing Doctor Finale, how well do you know him?' I did not reply. How well I knew Lester was not her business. 'Does he look like your father?'

I said I could see no resemblance, but when I put down the telephone I wondered. When I left home I had taken with me a photograph of Jacob, and now I compared it with one of Lester as Doctor Finale. At times it seemed to me there was no likeness, at others the two faces seemed to blend into each other and become one. I found Jennifer's scenes with Doctor Finale disturbing, especially those when the Doctor touched her and, on one occasion when she had made a mistake, hit her so that she fell and lay whimpering in a corner of the room. The director was pleased with the scene but Lester was concerned, said he hoped he hadn't hurt me. I replied that he couldn't possibly have hurt *me*, he would have hurt Jennifer, and since she had recovered enough to be in a car chasing a pair of grave-robbers a few minutes later, she had not been hurt. Lester laughed, but I'm not sure he understood what I meant, which was that Jennifer is one person, I am another.

When I rang Susan again three or four days later she surprised me by saying Jacob had hired a television and a video recorder. He had taped the last two *Doctor Finale* programmes, including the one in which Jennifer was knocked across the room, and played them again and again. She said he was beside himself, at one moment raging against my betrayal of him by putting him on the screen, the next saying he must protect me against the way I was being treated. She wanted me to come home and talk to him. I asked how she thought that would help. I was very calm.

'He believes this Doctor Finale is made up to look like him, and it's your doing.' I repeated that this was ridiculous. 'The men at the club all think it's a great joke, they've started calling him Doctor Finale. If you could explain to him—'

'There's nothing to explain.' But there was something I wanted to know. 'You saw the programmes, did you think she was good, Jennifer? Did she convince you?'

'Good? Oh yes, I suppose so.' She spoke in that strangled voice, as if she didn't mean it. 'I wish you would talk to him. He's not himself. He hates the television, but he sits in front of it playing those scenes with you in them, sometimes shouting at you and at the man. I'm afraid of what he'll do.'

I didn't take her seriously. I should have done. I said I had no intention of coming home or talking to Jacob. I repeated what I had said before: she should leave Jacob and come and live with me. That might have been awkward, because Lester had moved in with me, but I suppose I really knew she would never leave Jacob.

So I come to the last scene of the tragedy.

The episode in production was based on what was said to be an actual plot by the CIA to assassinate Castro by poisoning the wet suit he used. The intended victim here was a Middle East dictator who had already foiled several assassination attempts, the most recent being shown in a violent opening scene where two agents were caught trying to fix limpet bombs to the dictator's yacht and are then tortured to death. Doctor Finale, approached by the government, produces the plan for the poisoned wet suit, then gains the dictator's confidence by revealing it to him. The Doctor plots with the dictator to blow up the House of Commons and install a friendly prime minister. The dictator fancies Jennifer, and attempts to rape her. Doctor Finale, who has appeared to arrange the rape, breaks in before the dictator has his wicked way, shoots him with a poisoned dart from a cigarette lighter, and escapes with Jennifer in a submarine lurking off the coast, mission accomplished.

Tosh, with plenty of action, lots of nastiness, scenes with the dictator's other women, et cetera.

We were shooting a scene between the Doctor and Jennifer, in which he tells her she must go to the dictator's bedroom and do whatever he asks. Jennifer at first refuses but finally agrees, compelled by the mesmeric power of Doctor Finale's malevolent gaze. At one moment she says he wouldn't care if she was given to the guards to be raped and brutalized. She waits for him to contradict her. 'Would you care? Would you?' she asks, and he replies calmly: 'Not in the least.'

It was a difficult scene to do – not to mention the over-the-top dialogue – and Joe Frawley the director was on his fourth take when there was a lot of noise from the dark area at the back of the set. It sounded as if props were being knocked over, then there were voices. After that, silence. And then Jacob Pryde came out of the darkness on to the studio floor.

Joe said: 'Who the hell are you?' Then he was silent as

Jacob moved towards Lester. The revolver, that fatal revolver, was in his hand. Jacob said: 'You are Doctor Finale. You have corrupted my daughter.'

Lester muttered something about it being just a play, shrank away. Seeing the two together I recognized the likeness discovered by Jacob's friends. It was not just that they were physically of a size. The shape of the lean head, the bell-like ring of the voice and its contemptuous tone, the look that pierced the personality of the person it was aimed at and punctured self-confidence and self-belief – that look to which I had been exposed daily during my most susceptible years – those were the similarities I recognized. There was this difference, that Lester was an actor assuming such qualities, while in Jacob they were real.

I knew what I had to do. 'Jacob,' I said. 'Father.'

He turned. That gaze of fire and ice was bent on me. 'I have come to take you home,' he said, and I replied that I would come home. I said he should give me the revolver. He came very close to me, held out the blue, shining thing, and I took it. His arms were spread wide, wide as those of a fallen angel, as I moved into his embrace. But then, as he looked over my shoulder, he must have seen Lester again. He shouted something incoherent about corruption and saving me and struggled to get the revolver. I knew why he wanted it, to kill Lester – I suppose in a way that would have been to kill himself – and I did my best to keep hold of it when I felt his hand on mine. The rest of them seemed to stay still, like figures in a tableau, as Jacob and I struggled. I heard a crack, another crack. I could not have said where it came from. Then Jacob sighed, and said something again about our going home together. And that was all. It seemed somehow right that he should have died in my arms – or was it in Jennifer's arms? Now that I think about it afterwards, I believe he really was Doctor Finale.

*

'Interesting, but I'm afraid not very satisfactory,' Dr Margetson said. Her eyes behind the large square glasses were gentle as a gazelle's. 'The idea of suggesting to patients that they should write about the experiences in the outer world that have brought them here is to see how near they get to facing what actually happened.'

'Does that really matter?' the visitor asked.

On Dr Margetson's desk there was a telephone, a diary pad, a paperweight in the shape of a lion's head, and a jar of red and yellow roses. She paused for a moment as if giving the visitor's novel idea consideration before she answered. 'Oh yes. Yes, I think it matters if they are unable to accept reality.' Her voice was delicate, light, comforting, although the words were not. 'Elvira is happy here at Fernley Park. She has made friends, I don't think she really wants to leave. It may even be possible to use her acting abilities in the Christmas play.'

'Nobody can like being shut up.'

'We try to make patients feel they are not shut up but cared for. But in any case – you've read this?' She indicated the exercise book written in a round, almost childish hand. 'Or rather, you've read a typed copy of it. What did you think?'

'It's very vivid. And quite clear, quite coherent.'

'But not accurate.'

'Oh yes, I thought so. Leaving home, getting out of the window—'

'But not about the reason for leaving. Elvira didn't leave because her father smacked her face. Nor because she was bored with what she learned about the book trade. In our conversations, long friendly conversations in which Elvira spoke freely, with no constraint or inducement, she told me of the many occasions when her father sexually abused her in the extension or library, whichever you call it. And Elvira consented, when she was a girl she was in love with her father. He was a handsome man, and she liked handsome

14

men. Then she fully realized what she was doing and felt a revulsion from it—'

'There is no proof, no proof anything happened at all. It's only what she says now. She said nothing at the time.'

Softly Dr Margetson said: 'And you never asked questions?'

'Why should I have done?' Susan Pryde's hands were clasped tightly. 'If there had been any proof—'

'Positive proof is often lacking in such matters. But we know, you and I, that Elvira was capable of deceit. And that she could be vicious. What she says here about your own tragedy is not the truth.'

Susan Pryde had been sitting, as she always tried to do, with the good side of her face turned towards Dr Margetson, but now she moved to show the waxen half of her features with their curious smiling sneer. 'It was an accident. I have always said so.'

The doctor's voice was dulcet. 'I don't mean to criticize you. But Elvira is not telling the truth. She says she was four or five years old, and perhaps playing with a doll. In fact she was eight, and perhaps already being molested.'

'It was all long ago. I've tried to put it out of my mind.'

'Elvira says you tried to stop her going into the library one day, perhaps because you suspected what happened there. There was an argument. She caught hold of the pan of fat and threw it in your face.'

'Why should you believe her? It's her word against mine.'

'I believe what she tells me, that she felt the need to atone for what she had done. That was partly why she telephoned so often. For that, and to have news of her father. He had never got over her departure, longed for her to come back. Isn't that so?'

'Perhaps.'

Miriam Margetson's gaze was friendly through the

15

square lenses. 'But he wanted the girl he had known, not the woman who appeared on a TV screen. So he destroyed the television.' She waited for a comment, but none came. 'He wanted to resume their relationship, something Elvira contemplated with horror at the same time that she desired it.'

'This is all something you are inventing.'

'Did you notice her hints about Lester? First that she knew him well, then the casual remark that he had moved in with her. He was a replacement for the father she loved and feared.'

'She happened to mention him, that's all. You make the worst of everything.'

Dr Margetson shook her head. 'Such remarks are never accidental, they have meaning. And so does what she says about the final scene, blending fact with invention. It's true your husband went to the studio with the idea that he could persuade or force Elvira to give up her work as an actress and return to him. And she agreed, so why should he want to fire the revolver?'

'To hurt the actor, Lester Morton, Doctor Finale.'

'Why should he do that when he thought Elvira had agreed to return with him? Is it really likely that the shots that killed him were fired by accident? Elvira says that when his arms closed on her she tried to keep hold of the revolver. And she did keep hold, her prints were on it.'

'It was the pressure of his hand that fired the shots.' Now Susan looked steadily, full face, at the doctor. 'I want my daughter home again. To live with me. Perhaps to resume her career.'

'I have to remind you that it was to avoid the trauma of appearing in court, with all it would have entailed, that Elvira became a voluntary patient here at Fernley Park.'

'Until she might be ready for release. That was three years ago.'

'She is not ready yet.'

'Let me judge for myself. It's more than a year since I saw her. I want to see my daughter.'

'As you wish.' The doctor picked up the telephone, murmured words. Her gentle eyes looked at Susan sympathetically.

Any doubt Susan Pryde felt about her daughter's health was dispelled by the sight of her. She wore a bright print dress, her bare arms were brown, she was smiling. A uniformed nurse stood beside the door. Elvira's voice was clear and high as she said: 'Miriam, I didn't know I was going to see you this afternoon.' She stopped. 'Who's this?'

She shrank back as Susan came towards her and said: 'It's me. Your mother.'

'No.' Elvira shook her head. 'You're ugly. My mother isn't ugly. Ask my father, he knows she's not ugly.'

Dr Margetson said: 'Elvira, be quiet and listen. Your mother wants—'

Elvira shrieked 'No' again, picked up the paperweight and threw it at Susan. There was a tinkle of broken glass as it hit a picture on the wall. Elvira moaned with distress, launched herself at Dr Margetson. They grappled for a moment, then the nurse pinned Elvira's arms behind her back and took her away.

The doctor retrieved her glasses, which had been knocked off. 'You see.'

'Is she often like that?'

'She lives in the present, which is Fernley Park, some other patients, me. She has eliminated the past. But if she is to leave here she must come to terms with it, remember it as it was.' She tapped the exercise book. 'This was a trial run. It is disappointing but we shall try again, perhaps in a different form. One day she will be ready to come out. But not yet.'

'She likes you.'

'Affection is often transferred. One must be careful not

to reject it. But also not to accept too completely. If you understand me.' She permitted herself a small smile.

'You believe she did this to my face, killed her father. Those things are not true. I *know* that, I tell you.' She turned the waxen side of her face to the doctor, the lip curled in its sneer.

'You are her mother. I respect your feelings.'

Susan Pryde's voice rose. 'You've institutionalized her, turned her into a zombie. You're the guilty one.'

'Perhaps it helps you to think so. I'm glad you've seen Elvira.' Dr Margetson picked up the lion's head paper-weight, replaced it on the desk. 'And whatever you think, no harm has been done. Except, of course, for a little broken glass.'

In the Bluebell Wood

Lance could not remember a time before he knew about King Arthur, the Knights of the Round Table, and the fact that he had been named after the most famous of them. The bluebell wood too had its place in this. It was his father who told him the stories, about the coming of Arthur, the beauty of Guinevere and her love of Lancelot. At first the stories were from a big book called the *Morte D'Arthur*, but then they came from poems, poems called the *Idylls of the King* written by a man named Tennyson, which was his father's surname, and as he learned his own.

In adolescence, thinking back, he remembered being in bed, fingers twitching the sheets, his father's face above him uttering passionately words he did not quite understand – *honour*, *chivalry* – and phrases that stayed in his mind even though he did not understand their meaning – 'live pure, speak true, right wrong, follow the King – else, wherefore born?' There was nothing in the poems about a bluebell wood, yet when he closed his eyes after the readings he quite distinctly saw himself, Lancelot, riding with Guinevere, dismounting at a stile, then walking hand in hand with her down a grassy path to the dimness of a wood carpeted with bluebells . . . And when he opened his eyes the words flowed round him still:

> *Many a bard, without offence,*
> *Has linked our names together in his lay,*
> *Lancelot, the flower of bravery, Guinevere*
> *The pearl of beauty*

The face of the story-teller loomed large above him, eyes magnified by round spectacles. He knew the rough feel of Army cloth on his bare arm, the smell of tobacco. His father was home on leave during the war. What was the war, why did his father wear a uniform and not armour, what did he do when he left home again, did he follow the King?

Nothing like that, his mother said. Anyway, she added laughing, if Lionel did follow the King he'd soon lose sight of him. 'Your father's blind as a bat without his glasses. He does hush-hush work.'

'What's hush-hush?'

'Secret. Work that keeps him away. Very important.'

'For the King?'

'I suppose you could say that. For King and country.'

They lived on the fringe of London, in an area that had missed almost all the wartime bombing. They had a little red-brick house with a tiny front garden and one at the back that was a little bigger. The house next door was just the same, and the one next door to that, and so on down the road. 'Only way to tell 'em apart is by numbers,' his mother Esme said. 'Know what we are?' she asked neighbours. 'Rabbits in hutches, that's what.'

'Good job we don't breed like 'em.'

'You can take precautions.'

They went off into fits of laughter. Esme was small, dark, quick moving. The neighbour, whose husband was fighting somewhere in Italy, was named Louise. They saw a lot of each other. When Lance came home from the school that was just three minutes' walk away, Louise would often be in the kitchen. Esme got his tea and they sat with him while he ate it, both smoking so that the room became blue with it, and talking incomprehensibly. He imagined Lancelot riding through those blue mists, freeing a fair maiden, then meeting Guinevere, they crossed the stile . . . Fragments of phrases came through to him.

'Dead and alive hole . . . see more life in a factory . . . you got a kid you got a millstone round your neck . . .'

His father came home on weekend leave from the hush-hush job quite often, and read from the *Idylls* about Gareth and Lynette, Merlin and Vivien, and what he loved most, Lancelot and Guinevere. Lying in bed, waiting for his father to come upstairs, he heard voices raised, his mother's sometimes almost a shriek.

It was when his father was at the hush-hush job that the visitor came. He was there when Lance came back from school, a tall smiling man who wore a much smarter uniform than his father's, and one with stars which the boy knew meant he was an officer, while his father had only the stripes of a sergeant. The officer's name was Pierre, and Esme said he belonged to the Free French. Pierre made pennies and a shilling come out of his ears, and gave them to Lance. Then Esme said she'd arranged for him to have tea and play with Tim Collins, who lived a few doors down the road. The arrangement was unusual, almost unknown.

'I don't want to.' He began to cry.

Esme's temper was short. 'You'll do as you're told. You're going out to tea, is that a reason to be a cry baby?'

'Look here.' Pierre produced another shilling from his ear. 'Why don't you and your friend Tim see what you can buy with this?'

When he was home again his mother said: 'I was ashamed of you, crying just because you'd been asked out to tea.' He made no reply. 'Did you like Pierre?'

'Don't know.'

'He's just a friend. Of Louise's really. No need to mention him to your father. Did you hear me?' He nodded. 'Say yes when you're spoken to.'

'Yes.'

He said nothing to his father, even though he saw Pierre again more than once – just leaving as he came home from school, in the kitchen where he made jokes when they had tea together, once coming out of the bathroom wearing only shirt and pants. Did Lance understand what was happening? That was a question he never asked himself later on. At the time he was simply puzzled when Tim Collins, who had never been a friend of his, said his mother was having it off with a frog. Having what off? he wondered, and he had only seen pictures of frogs.

But although he said nothing he did compare the round-shouldered goggle-eyed figure in a uniform that never seemed to fit properly with upright, trim, smiling Pierre, whose trousers had a crease of knife-edge sharpness, and who could make shillings come out of his ears. Then suddenly the war was over, there was a big party in their road with lots of food, including things he had never seen, like bananas, all set out on trestle tables, dancing and drinking. Pierre was seen no more, someone said he had gone back to France, and good riddance. Esme went around red eyed, and shorter tempered than usual. And Lionel Tennyson, no longer Sergeant Tennyson, was demobbed, came home, went back to his work in the Ministry. Yes, he said to Lance, the war was really over.

'And we won. We beat the bad men like Sir Modred, the good knights won.' By this time Lance was reading the *Idylls* himself, knew some of the exciting bits by heart.

'The good knights won,' his father echoed. They were in the bow-windowed living room. On the walls were reproductions of Victorian pictures, one showing the passing of Arthur, another Lancelot and Guinevere. He stood, in full armour, looking at his drawn sword, she knelt and gazed at him yearningly, her long fair hair around her face and falling to her waist, feet showing below the pure white of her robe. A silver-plated figure of King Arthur stood on the mahogany sideboard, drawing the magic sword Excalibur from its scabbard.

Yes, his father said, but it was not like King Arthur. 'Bombs instead of swords nowadays. More's the pity.'

'But the stories are all really true, aren't they?'

'Oh yes, yes, yes.' His father became excited, as he had been when reading aloud about Lancelot's deeds as an unknown knight at a tournament. 'They are all true, and you must never forget them. That's why you were named Lancelot.' He still read to his son sometimes at night, until Esme said the boy was too old for that now, it just encouraged him to be childish.

Afterwards Lance remembered these years of adolescence as an idyll in his own life. His father went each day to the Ministry and he went to school, got good reports, came back, did his homework and then read a romantic story like *Kidnapped* or *Under the Red Robe*. Later, in bed, he read the *Idylls*. Afterwards he tried to remember something Esme had said that showed dissatisfaction with this life, which for her was one of keeping house and cooking, but could recall nothing. There were none of the arguments he had heard downstairs when he was a child, she was meticulous as ever in seeing that meals were cooked on time and in cleaning the house so that everything smelt of furniture polish.

Then one day she was gone. He came home to find tea on the table, bread and margarine, jam, scones she had made the previous day. He ate, washed up the things, settled down in the kitchen to his homework. When his father came home he said: 'Mum's out.' Mr Tennyson nodded, went upstairs, came down again five minutes later looking paler than usual, eyes behind thick glasses vacant as those of a fish. He sat down at the kitchen table, put his head in his hands, said to his son: 'She's taken all her things, everything. Gone.'

Lance was aware of his open mouth, closed it, said gone where? His father shook his head. 'When will she be coming back?'

'She isn't. You remember a man coming round two or three weeks ago selling vacuum cleaners, or trying to?' Lance nodded. 'She's gone off with him. With a vacuum cleaner salesman.'

Lance put an arm round his father's shoulder. 'We can manage. Until she comes back.'

'She hates me, she says so in the letter. She'll never come back.' He raised a face wet with tears.

Esme didn't come back. And Mr Tennyson was quite incapable of managing. He burned meat and undercooked vegetables, and since these were days before frozen foods they ate mostly out of tins. A woman who came in to do housework stole the few valuable things in the house, including the figure of King Arthur. Within a year the house had been sold and they moved into a small flat in the same area, but in a main road with lorries rattling by day and night. It was cheaper, less trouble, a cleaner came in a couple of hours each week, there was nothing much to steal. The Victorian prints of Arthur, Lancelot and Guinevere remained, although they looked out of place in the tiny living room. There was no garden, and Mr Tennyson loved gardening. One day Lance asked what the secret work was that his father had done in the war.

'Helping to decode German messages. I'm a statistician, you see, good at analysing sets of numbers and figures. I was one of a team. What we did was really quite important.'

He sensed that this was delicate ground. 'But no fighting?'

'No fighting. I wouldn't have been much good at it. Like you, I can't see very well.' And Lance, looking in the mirror, saw that his glasses were almost as thick as his father's, his face the same moon shape. So what was his father's job now at the Ministry, was it still important work?

'Not really. Mostly paperwork. Ordering materials for use in government contracts, then following them through, checking prices, keeping suppliers on their toes about delivery, making sure they don't overcharge. It's secure, you see, that's the great thing. When you're in the civil service you have a job for life. I'm not a do-er, you know, but I love the stories, and I wanted you to love them too. And of course there's my name, that made me read the poems first of all. I was called Lionel, and Lionel Tennyson was a great cricketer, captain of England. But I'm a reader, not a do-er. It was a kind of separate life for me.'

A separate life, a secret life. Perhaps that conversation was the beginning for Lance of the secret life in which he was somebody different from the awkward teenager who looked uneasily at the world through round spectacles, was shy with girls and no good at games. In the secret life Judy, who burst into laughter when he asked if she would like to go with him to a pop concert, said wistfully that she thought Lancelot was a beautiful name, and wished she was called Guinevere and not dull Judy. 'To me you will always be Guinevere,' he said as she leaned towards him, opening her lips for the kiss.

The closest of Lance's few friends at school was Rod Williams, who told all sorts of tales about his father's adventures as a scrap dealer. 'What's your father do?' Rod asked. 'Office job, isn't it, pen pushing?'

'Not really. It's hush-hush work.'

'But what's he *do*?'

'He's an agent.'

'What, MI5?'

'More secret. He's part of a very small group, they have to protect the Queen. The other Royals too, but the Queen especially. I'm not supposed to talk about it. Swear you won't tell anyone.'

Rod swore, but of course told his father. Later Lance showed Rod a newspaper photograph of the invasion of Suez, and said one of the background figures was his father.

'Thought you said he was protecting the Queen. What's this got to do with her?'

Lance realized he had made a mistake. 'That isn't all his group does. They've got other duties.'

Rod was a large youth with small eyes and a pig's upturned nose. 'My dad says you're making it all up. Just fairy stories, he says.'

'Your dad doesn't *know*.' But after that Lance gave up the stories about his father, who was becoming more and more absentminded, withdrawn into what Lance supposed were secret thoughts. In the evening, after supper, he switched on the television and sat staring at it with no apparent awareness of what he was watching.

He received few letters, but one morning a long envel- ope came, name and address typed. Mr Tennyson examined the postmark, turned over the envelope and looked at the back (Lance thought immediately of secret messages), slit it open, read the contents carefully, pushed aside his cereal, took off his glasses and wiped his eyes, spoke.

'Your mother. She's dead. A car accident. She was on her own. Apparently she'd been drinking.'

Lance felt nothing. It seemed to him an age ago that they had lived in the red-brick house with the front and back garden, that Pierre had made shillings come out of his ears, his father had come home on leave and read the *Idylls* to him. A curtain had been dropped in his mind, concealing that world as if it had never existed. Reality was here and now, the little flat where he lived, the school he would soon be leaving, and the secret world in which Judy/Guinevere entered the arms of Lancelot.

'I loved her, you know. In spite of everything I loved her. We were never divorced and I always hoped she would come back. I know it was my fault.' At that Lance was indignant. Esme had left her home and her child, how could it have been her husband's fault? Mr Tennyson shook his head. 'You don't understand, how could you? She was a kind of dream to me, and she didn't like dreamers.' He gave his son what almost seemed a glare through the pebbled glasses. 'What about you? You're leaving at the end of this term, what do you want to do?'

'I don't know. I don't want to go to a university. Something exciting.'

His father's laugh was a rusty caw. 'No money for a university, I can tell you that. Something exciting, that's stupid.'

'What you used to read to me, the *Idylls*, that was exciting.'

'That was reading, poetry. Very nice, but not real. Perhaps I shouldn't have – you must get started, that's the thing. I might be able to help.' For a moment Lance had a vision of his own place in that imaginary world in which his father was an agent, but the next words dispelled it. 'Customs and Excise.'

'What?'

'A Customs officer, good safe job. I'll make enquiries, might be able to pull some strings.'

And the strings were pulled, so that Lance became a member of HM Customs and Excise. There was a training period in which he learned what to look out for, the sort of travellers likely to have watches loaded on both arms, the likely drug stuffers and swallowers, the foolish innocents who thought they could break the rules just this once and showed awareness of it in their faces and gestures.

It sounded exciting, and he imagined scenes in which the secret life became reality. There would be a woman traveller, not exactly beautiful but elegant, stylish, the kind of woman whose very appearance left him tongue-tied. She walked through the 'Nothing To Declare' channel at the airport, cool and faintly disdainful. He asked her to open a case, and her raised eyebrows asked *Can you really mean it?*, but were then replaced by a panic-stricken *I may just have forgotten* . . . And then the opened case revealed – what? Something forgivable, an undeclared item from St Laurent, a small storehouse of scents, something on which she need not be taken to court.

Afterwards she was grateful, asked his name, was enchanted to know it was Lancelot, suggested a meeting – but at that point fantasy was checked, for there were strict rules about such matters and he was not sure that he wanted to break them. In any case the disdainful elegant ladies remained in his imagination. He encountered in his duties instead pathetic Africans or South Americans who carried drugs in stomach or rectum, or petty villains who travelled a lot by air on genuine business, and fancied their chances of getting drugs or watches through Customs as a kind of perk. Being a Customs officer at an airport, as he said to his father, was as dull a job as any other.

A few months after Lance began work Mr Tennyson took early retirement from the Ministry. Was the retirement purely voluntary, or had it been urged on him by his superiors? Either way, he showed unmistakable signs of a mental decline that was more than absentmindedness. He would go out shopping, wander off to a nearby park, sit there for an hour or two and return having forgotten to do the shopping. In the flat he let milk boil over on the stove, forgot to turn off a gas fire so that it burned all night, and almost caused a fire by leaving an electric iron on while watching television. At times he thought Esme was still alive and was coming back to live with them, so that he cleared a cupboard for her clothes and rearranged all the furniture. When Lance first got the Customs and Excise job he thought of looking for an apartment on his own, but it was borne in on him that this was not possible. He would have to look after his father, who although insisting that he was perfectly well (and seeming healthier than when he was at the Ministry) admitted to becoming absentminded.

Mr Tennyson's interest in the *Idylls* had lapsed after news of Esme's death, but it revived in retirement. He read biographies of Tennyson, and deluged Lance with quotations from the *Idylls*, most of them designed to dampen what he saw as his son's unhealthy yearning for excitement. Life, he said, was a great teacher, and he quoted: 'A young man will be wiser by and by.' Not only a great teacher, Life, but it cut you down to size. 'The dirty nurse, Experience, in her kind hath foul'd me' – Lance should remember that this had happened to his father in the sad loss of his wife. After he had gained experience he should look for a nice girl, and inevitably he quoted: 'In the spring a young man's fancy—'

Brutality was not in Lance's nature, but he came near to it then. 'And what would you do when I found a girl, live with us? My wife might have something to say about that.'

Nothing like that, Mr Tennyson said, adding with insufferable complacency: 'No need to worry, I can look after myself.' The obvious truth was that he couldn't.

But the problem didn't arise, because Elaine the fair maid of Astolat who died for the love of Lancelot, and Guinevere whom he loved guiltily, remained as much figures of the secret world as the disdainful woman traveller. Lance found it hard to know what to say to girls. When he looked in the glass a moon face stared back at him with eyes owlish behind the round glasses, and a head that wobbled so much on its thin neck that it seemed likely to fall off. What girl could fancy someone who looked like that?

On the other hand it was true that Rod, who was certainly not handsome, pulled plenty of girls. He chatted them up when they stopped at the stall he had in the local market, where he sold all sorts of odds and ends including stuff bought by his father the scrap merchant. 'Nothing to it,' Rod said, little pig eyes twinkling. 'Couple of drinks, bit of chat, and bang you're in.'

That was all right perhaps for Rod, who had his own

place, but Lance couldn't possibly have shocked his father by taking a girl back to their flat. Rod immediately said go back with him, Lance could have the bedroom, he wasn't fussy, he and his girl would manage on the sitting room sofa. Got to get your leg over some time, Rod said, plenty of nookie about, no need to pay prossies for it. The sly sideways glance he gave when saying that was justified. Lance had been with prostitutes. Such encounters at least involved no chatting up, but although as Rod put it he got his leg over, these brief encounters were not satisfying. After them he felt ashamed, for they seemed a betrayal of the tall fair slender girl he met in the secret life, the girl to whom no words had to be spoken, no explanations made. They met, crossed the stile, walked hand in hand towards the darkness of the wood and the brightness of the bluebells that made a carpet within it, and then lay down together.

It was through Rod that the secret life and Lance's everyday world became one. Rod played for a pub darts team, and occasionally Lance went along to watch. Two girls were with Rod, one fair, one dark.

'Del, you know Lance,' Rod said. 'Gwyn, this is Lance I was telling you about, works in Customs. Want to watch out for him, he's a tiger, so they tell me.' General laughter. 'You should see him in his uniform, he's hot stuff.'

'I can imagine,' the dark girl said, not joking, as if she meant it.

Lance bought a round. The dark girl spoke to him. 'Rod was on about you, said you were dead clever only you don't talk much. Why's that?'

'Nothing to say, I expect.'

'Doesn't stop me, Del, does it? You either.' She laughed, showing regular teeth. 'But you, Lance, I bet you're deep. Is he deep, Rod?'

'Deep as the deep blue sea,' Rod said. At this too there was laughter, and Lance did not feel it was directed at him. When the dark girl went on to ask what he was thinking about he said: 'All right, I'll tell you. Your name, Gwyn. Why are you called that, what's it short for?'

'Nosy, aren't we? OK, I don't mind telling, it's Gwyneth. Gwyneth Lewis, there's Welsh for you. What about Lance, what sort of name is that?'

For once, strangely, he did not mind saying his name was Lancelot, even added that he thought Gwyn might have been short for Guinevere.

'That's King Arthur, I know about him, saw the film. She was Arthur's wife. But then she and Lancelot—' She looked at Lance, burst out laughing.

A couple of hours and more than a couple of drinks later, the darts match lost, Rod said to him at the bar: 'You're well away there, boy, Gwyn fancies you.'

'She does?' Rod closed one little eye. But it still seemed incredible to Lance, and in any case where could he take Gwyn, who was dark instead of fair but still might really be Guinevere? He was not sure he had enough money for a hotel. But that turned out to be no problem at all. When they left the pub she took his arm and said: 'My place, all right?'

What followed was shocking, exciting and exhausting, quite unlike the brief encounters he had known. Just after midnight he remembered his father, said he must telephone.

'You what?'

'I must tell my father. He'll be worried.'

She stared at him, and for a moment he thought she was going to tell him to get out, go home. Instead she put up a hand, stroked his cheek. 'You're funny. OK, there's the phone.'

His father's voice was first indignant, then petulant. Did Lance know the time, surely he could have rung earlier, where was he, why couldn't he come home? At the end he said Lance was unkind and thoughtless, and put down the telephone without saying goodbye.

In the morning she made toast and coffee, then went back to bed. He asked if she was out of work.

'I'm on and off, and this week's off. I do jobs for a travel agency, escorting groups, mostly Spain and Portugal. Bloody hard work, don't let anyone tell you different. Next week I'm taking some old dears to Amsterdam, coach tour.' She laughed. 'Last time I mislaid one, turned out he'd gone to the casino, won a bagful of money, got beaten up, landed in hospital. They blamed me, wouldn't you know?'

When Lance had dressed he didn't know what he should say. 'Can I . . .' He began again. 'I mean, I don't suppose you're free . . .'

'Thought you'd never ask. Free as air, Lance. Funny name, but I like it, reminds me of something, wonder what it can be?'

'What – oh, I see.' He blushed, and she laughed. She did not speak the language of Guinevere, and she was not like the woman who inhabited the secret world, but her face coalesced in the image of the fair-haired Guinevere who knelt at Lancelot's feet.

When he stood in the Customs hall and sat in the canteen the Gwyn who walked beside him in the secret world, who crossed the stile and went down the path with him to the bluebell wood was Gwyn who had been transformed into Guinevere.

Each evening after work he met her. Twice they went out with Rod and his Delia, but he liked it best when they were on their own. They saw a movie, went to a concert, ate in cheap restaurants, and talked – or for the most part Lance talked and she listened, for his diffidence had gone, he had become eloquent, talking of King Arthur and the *Idylls* and Lancelot's love for Guinevere. And they went to bed, about which she was more urgent than he. The physical act offered a kind of fulfilment of his worship of Guinevere, yet something about it seemed to him messy and coarse, unlike love in the secret world. There you kissed and fondled, but there was none of the sticky glueing of mouth to mouth, nor the moans and subdued shrieks that Gwyn uttered, sounds that had no place in a Tennysonian idyll.

After that first night they spent only evenings together. Mr Tennyson grumbled about his late return to the flat, but accepted Lance's explanation about being short-handed and working extra hours, and one of his colleagues at work said he seemed almost human, instead of going through the motions like a robot. Only Gwyn showed dissatisfaction when he left her. 'You don't want to stay, that it?' she asked. Lance said his father, an old man, couldn't be left alone to look after himself. She shook her head.

'You got to look after number one in this world. And have fun. Still, we do that, don't we?' He said yes, although the physical business was something he found increasingly a problem, and having fun was not an adequate description of the joy he had in the secret world which he could create even in the canteen or walking along the street – but most of all in bed alone at night when coarse-speaking Gwyn became sweet Guinevere. He was transported into that life even in her presence now, so that one evening she tapped his forehead and said: 'Anyone home? Didn't hear, did you? I said next week I can't see you, taking these old dears to Amsterdam. Not that the red light district there will do any of 'em much good.' Her laugh was loud. 'We'll be back Saturday though, I can see you Sunday. Thing is, are you on that weekend?' He said he was.

'I want you to stop me, check my bags.' She went on quickly. 'Tell you for why. My boss is coming on the trip, nosy bastard, one of the other girls has got it in for me, told him I'm bringing in stuff I shouldn't, know what I mean? So my young brother Billy, he wants a watch, I'm going to buy one out there, go through the "Something To Declare" channel, pay the duty, OK?'

'Yes, but I don't see—'

'You look at the rest of my gear, check it, give it the

OK, show the little fat bastard that's my boss where he gets off trying to climb into bed with me. Which is all he wants, I may say. I hate fat men, starving lean hungry ones are my meat.' She giggled. 'Just think what Sunday'll be like when I'm back, I'll have been good for a week.'

He hardly missed her physical presence in the week while she was away. She existed in the secret world, transformed into the Guinevere of the *Idylls* by a chaste radiant glow that surrounded her. He imagined her watching him fighting in the tournament, telling him that she loved him even though she knew this love to be a betrayal, but the scene most persistent in his mind was that when they walked along the path to the bluebell wood, and there lay down together in a tree's green shade. It was the world he had so often read about made real, that world

> *Where falls not hail, or rain, or any snow,*
> *Nor ever wind blows loudly, but it lies*
> *Deep-meadow'd, happy, fair with orchard lawns*
> *And bowery hollows crown'd with summer sea*

Mr Tennyson cheered up no end at having his son home every evening, managed some shopping and cooking successfully, and said it was just like old times. The Chief Customs Officer at the airport, on the other hand, said Lance wanted to wake his ideas up, he looked like a tit in a trance, and it was true that as he stood with a couple of other officers, smart in their uniforms, he absented himself from the passengers who streamed past looking happy, eager or anxious, pushing and wheeling bags and cases.

He was absent in the world of Lancelot, or only half-present, when a voice said: 'Got the receipt somewhere,' and he was suddenly aware of Gwyn before him, Gwyn pushing a trolley that held a suitcase and a holdall. She wore a dark-blue raincoat and a jaunty blue hat with a red feather in it. Behind her a fellow Customs officer, whose carrot-coloured hair had brought him the name Red, mouthed something silently and grinned. There was no sign of the little fat boss, who had perhaps gone through the 'Nothing To Declare' channel with the rest of her party.

Lance looked at the watch she showed him in its case, and at the receipt, got a list to check the duty payable, tapped the case and holdall and asked her to open them.

Gwyn looked at Red in mock despair, he shook his head sympathetically. She unlocked the case, zipped open the holdall, over-dramatically gave him her handbag, stood back.

Lance's fingers moved lightly among jacket and skirts, underwear, powder, lipstick, scent. He replaced them, and was about to zip up the holdall when beneath his fingertips he felt the hint of an obstacle, nothing more than a rucked up bit of lining perhaps, except that no lining should have existed there. He looked up to find Gwyn's large dark eyes staring into his own challengingly, expectantly. His fingers moved further, more carefully, over the holdall's surface, and he knew the obstacle was not a natural one.

There was then a moment of uncertainty for him, a moment when Gwyn's lips – could they ever have been Guinevere's? – curved in a confident smile. Then the smile was broken, the whole shape of her face seemed to change and splinter as he picked up her bags and said they would need to examine them more closely. She made for him, claws out and spitting words never used by Guinevere, and Red had to help him restrain her.

The velour-lined false pocket in the holdall contained uncut diamonds, emeralds and sapphires. As Red said wonderingly, it was hard to see why the silly bitch played it the way she did, calling attention to herself over the watch. If she'd gone through the 'Nothing To Declare' channel she'd have had a chance of getting through, though they always took a hard look at couriers in charge of groups. As it was, Gwyneth Lewis was duly charged, and released on bail.

'You're silent tonight,' Mr Tennyson said. 'Something on your mind?'

'Betrayal.'

'What's that? Something from the *Idylls*?'

'Not from the *Idylls*. I'm going out.'

He wandered aimlessly about the streets, found himself outside the pub where he met Gwyn, went in. Rod was at the bar, a glass raised. Beer sprayed from his mouth when he saw Lance. 'You got a nerve,' he said, 'coming in here, showing your face.'

'I don't understand.'

'Gwyn gave it you straight enough, didn't she? Asked you to check her stuff, what you think she did that for? So you could shop her? All you had to do was charge duty on the watch, pass her through, there was a century in it for you. Woulda been more next time. Whatsa matter, more stupid than you look, are you?' Rod's snout was very close to Lance. 'You landed everybody in it, me included for making the intro. And you should look out, she's Corney Barrow's girl.'

Corney Barrow was well known locally, a villain reputed to have a hand in everything from acting as a fence to selling dope. 'You mean—'

'I said I made the intro, Corney wanted an in at the airport, I said you could be useful getting stuff through. Now you dropped his girl in it. You want to watch yourself, mate. If I were you I'd move out of the area for a while.' Lance said that was not possible because of his father. 'Suit yourself,' Rod said, and turned away.

So he had been betrayed by Gwyn, and betrayed her in his turn, because he had been forced to realize she was

Gwyneth Lewis and not Guinevere. But as he went from one pub to another, drinking whisky to which he was unused, the image of Gwyn faded and was replaced wholly by that of Guinevere, looking as in the picture so lovingly, so yearningly, at Lancelot. The lustre of her fair hair was with him as he left the last pub, and three of them came out after him. He saw light flash on steel, heard only faintly the voice say something about a present from Corney. There was a pain in his side, a dull but deepening pain, and he felt himself truly Sir Lancelot, suffering as 'a spear prick'd sharply his own cuirass, and the head pierc'd thro' his side, and there snapt, and remain'd.' Lancelot then cried out her name: 'Guinevere,' he cried. 'The flower of all the west and all the world.' He hardly felt what seemed the hoofbeats trampling and kicking him, and in his last moments was aware only that Guinevere had taken his hand and was leading him down to the peace of the bluebell wood where they would rest for ever.

Et In
Arcadia Ego

Gerald was brought up in Arcadia, which was no doubt a problem. But he had more difficulties than that.

Arcadia was the name given by the builder to an estate of what were called in the brochure individually designed houses for top-class executives, combining the peace and grace of country living with all the nearby facilities of a market town, plus an hourly train service to London. The development, of no more than thirty houses, was snapped up before they were built, but their popularity prompted a second eager entrepreneur to acquire several adjacent acres on which was built in due course Greater Arcadia. The original Arcadians thus found themselves part of a much bigger complex, and one less socially desirable than they had envisaged. The original Arcadia had been a couple of miles out of town, but its much larger offshoot plus the shops and petrol stations set up to serve it meant that the town merged almost indistinguishably into Arcadian country. But there were still green fields and country walks around, and it was said that nobody had ever sold a house in the Arcadias at anything but a handsome profit.

Arcadia, then, was still more or less Arcadian. Until the Soft Shoe Rapist came.

Mr Burke worked in London in a ministry, something to do with what was called social development, and he had risen in the gradual, almost inevitable Civil Service way to become quite important. Very important? No, not that, a secondary figure who as he sometimes said was subject to the demands of his lord and master, the Minister. He had left a comfortable London suburb and come to Arcadia at the urging of his wife Pearl, who had aspirations to a more gracious way of life. And Pearl did find Arcadian life more gracious, although it worried her that so many of the other Arcadians (not Greater Arcadians, an inferior breed) had swimming pools and Jacuzzis that the Burkes could not afford. She was trying to persuade her husband that a Jacuzzi, at least, was an essential adjunct to Arcadian living when she ran her car into a tree and died instantly. Gerald, three years old at the time, was in the car with her, and insisted when the police arrived that his mother was asleep.

Up to that time Mr Burke had hardly been aware of Gerald's existence. He saw the child only for a couple of minutes in the morning before taking the London train, and by the time he returned in the evening Gerald was being put to bed. Pearl's death, however, made him uncomfortably aware that he was responsible for this rather large three-year-old child. A few months of life with a housekeeper worried about what she called Gerald's persistent naughtiness, which she tried to cure by smacking him frequently on the head, arms and legs with a ruler, convinced him that this wouldn't do. He married Emerald, exchanging, as he said in one of his few but often-repeated jokes, one jewel for another.

Emerald was a secretary in the Ministry, and already had a son of Gerald's age named Gavin, the outcome of an affair that had ended even before Gavin was born. She was looking for security rather than romance or social status, and rightly thought that in Mr Burke she had found it. When she first visited Arcadia she held out her arms to Gerald, who backed away. Later on the same day the boys quarrelled when playing a game together and Gerald, who was much the larger, got astride Gavin and began to bang his head on the floor. Emerald said Gerald seemed rather uncontrolled, and Mr Burke said she would soon lick him into shape. Then he spoke to his son. 'Gerald, this is your new mother. Come and kiss her.' At that Gerald ran out of the room.

Emerald did not lick Gerald into shape, had no desire to lick anybody into shape. She was a simple, easy-going woman whose voice retained traces of her East End origins. She thought she had made a lucky marriage, enjoyed life in Arcadia, and hardly noticed the whispers among those Mr Burke regarded as his friends that he had certainly taken a step or two down in the social scale with his second marriage. Emerald knew the importance of keeping her man happy, and the not unrelated problem of keeping her figure. She looked after Gavin, the second star round which her life revolved, and would have looked after Gerald and helped him with homework as she did Gavin, but Gerald wouldn't let her. Once she had, unfortunately, suggested a wrong answer to a question about history, and when he came home the next afternoon he tore up his exercise book and threw it at her. After that she gave up. 'When he wants help he'll ask for it,' she said to her husband, and Mr Burke nodded agreement.

As the years went by it became obvious, or should have been obvious, that Gerald needed help from somebody. The difference between his abilities and those of Gavin became more marked with every year. They both went to the primary school in town and then to the state-aided grammar, and Gavin at once showed his aptitude and eagerness for learning, while Gerald was never better than sluggish, regarded by some teachers as backward, by others as deliberately lazy. Gavin won prizes for best essay, most original drawing, biggest contribution to class harmony. Gerald won no prizes at all, and was consistently near the bottom of every class.

The differences extended to their appearance. Gavin was small, neat and tidy, Gerald an outsize boy, six foot tall at thirteen and bulky with it. His clothes always seemed too small for him, buttons somehow became torn off his jackets, his shoes were sometimes unlaced, his lank hair all over the place. The only area in which Gerald might have excelled was sport. His reactions were too slow for him to get into the cricket or football teams, but he was anchor man in the tug-of-war competition and won the heavyweight boxing, although in the following year he refused to go in for it. 'What do I want to hit him for, he's done nothing to me,' he said to the sports master, who was tickled enough to tell Mr Burke.

Gerald's father was not tickled at all. He set out to give his son some friendly advice about the need for competition in life, but found him so unresponsive that, most unusually for him, he began to shout. 'You're ready to let everybody walk all over you, is that it, is that what you mean to do in life?'

Gerald shuffled his size twelve shoes. 'Don't know.'

'Don't know, you *ought* to know, you've got to stand up for yourself, not let people walk all over you. Otherwise you'll end up as a crossing sweeper.' Afterwards he spoke to Emerald. 'I don't want to be hard on the boy. Has he got any school-friends?' She shook her head. 'No friends, doesn't work at school, sits up in his room reading comics or wearing those earphones and listening to pop music. It's not natural, he's got no interest in anything. I tell you, Gavin's more like my son than my own flesh and blood is.'

Emerald laughed. 'You're so impatient, it's not like you. You just see, I think he's a late developer, he'll do something that surprises you one day.'

There was no sign of Gerald doing anything surprising at the end of his schooldays. Gavin got a scholarship to Oxford. Gerald did get a job, indeed several jobs, but kept none of them for long. He was an assistant in a record shop, served behind the counter in the local fast food restaurant, worked on a lathe in a shoe factory, did odd jobs in a timber yard, and was a rider for a messenger service. He puttered in and out of town on a scooter wearing a mauve woollen hat to which he became much attached. He had no girlfriends, and went on reading the comics that most of the boys he knew at school had given up at the age of fourteen. Emerald was indulgent as ever, but Gerald's jobs and his appearance fulfilled all Mr Burke's worst fears. He could hardly bear to look at the boy.

The thing that infuriated him more than anything else was that Gerald seemed quite unaware of the ludicrous figure he cut among the neat lawns, gleaming Volvos, Vauxhalls and sports Escorts, and the designer jeans of his young contemporaries in Arcadia. When Gavin came home and brought friends with him the appearance of Gerald, shambling and awkward, dressed in baggy and not very clean trousers, sitting on a sofa reading comics in which heroes endowed with miraculous powers got the better of villains armed with germ bombs and remote control devices that could trigger off the destruction of cities, was almost more than Mr Burke could bear. Something, he said, must be done. Supposing he was set up in the town with a small flat of his own, how would that do? Perhaps Gavin could speak to him?

So Gavin spoke but, as he had warned his mother and step-father in advance, without effect. 'He really didn't seem to understand what I was talking about,' he reported. 'He says this is his home, he doesn't want to leave it. I think he'd be lost in a place of his own, he wouldn't look after himself. He says if you don't want him to read comics downstairs he'll keep them in his room.'

'What about your friends, what do they say?'

'Don't get me wrong when I say they think he's a joke. But they don't mind him, nor do I.' Gavin hesitated. 'I think you should accept him as a sort of force of nature.'

Emerald's eyes filled with tears, and she said they mustn't send Gerald away, it would be too cruel.

So Gerald stayed. He was now six foot five and very broad, with enormous hands. Shoes had to be specially made to fit him.

Then came the Soft Shoe Rapist.

He appeared in Greater Arcadia, visiting three houses within a month. He was evidently adept at climbing drain-pipes and getting on to roofs, his means of access being through windows left marginally or wide open on the upper floors of houses. He wore a mask, was clothed in black, and threatened his victims either with a revolver or a large curved knife. All the attacks were made late at night. His first two victims were young women with small children whose husbands were away, something that suggested knowledge of the people in the houses, or careful study of their habits. The third victim was in Arcadia itself, a middle-aged woman who slept in another room from her husband. He woke, however, entered his wife's bedroom, and was stabbed twice in the ensuing fight. He was rushed to hospital, and for a week was on the critical list, but recovered.

Because the rapist operated in the dark, descriptions were necessarily vague, but the victims agreed that he was big, with powerful hands. He spoke in a soft hissing voice, and moved soundlessly. A footprint of a light-weight hi-tech shoe was found at the bottom of one drainpipe he had climbed, and the press christened him the Soft Shoe Rapist.

A Guardian Committee was set up to organize the protection of Arcadia. Its chairman was a local car dealer named Frampton, and one of the members was the owner of the timber yard where Gerald had worked, whose name was Tilsley Williams. It was Williams who came round to the Burkes' house and suggested that Gerald should join the committee. Gerald was out, and he saw Mr Burke who stared at him when Williams made the request.

'There's nobody from this part of the estate has joined the committee,' Williams said. Mr Burke did not care for Arcadia to be lumped in with the much inferior houses of Greater Arcadia as 'the estate', but he did not comment. 'And he's a good strong lad, Gerald. And willing, or was when he worked for us, we were sorry to lose him.' At this Mr Burke winced. The very idea of his son working in a timber yard, and of this bristly-moustached little tradesman talking about him familiarly, was odious. 'Course we'd like it if you'd join us yourself, but I don't suppose you can spare the time.' The sarcasm in Williams's voice was kept just within the limits of politeness. 'Trouble is, we're all chiefs and no Indians, if you take my meaning. Gerry'd be useful helping around, delivering rotas and such. That's if he felt inclined.'

Mr Burke said distantly that he would speak to his son when he came in, and let Mr Williams know the result. He talked to Emerald, who was all in favour of the idea, and then Gerald, who listened to him carefully, then said, 'He's a bad man, isn't he?'

'What, the—' Mr Burke could not bring himself to use the ghastly media term. 'Yes, very bad.'

'He ought to be stopped.'

'Of course, but—' He checked himself again. 'Some people would think catching this sort of man is best left to the police.'

'They haven't caught him. The good men have to join together to catch the bad ones.'

'I don't think they expect you to catch him. From what I can make out they want you as a kind of messenger boy.'

'I don't mind about that.' Gerald smiled. He had a sweetly innocent smile, or so Emerald said. Mr Burke simply felt he would like to knock some sense into the boy's head.

So Gerald became a member of the Guardian Committee, which operated enthusiastically for the next few

45

weeks. Frampton had lapel badges printed for committee members saying 'Guardian', and Gerald wore his all the time on his jacket or pullover. A roster was organized by which Guardians in couples took turns keeping watch in Arcadia and Greater Arcadia throughout the night. All of them were men, something commented on unfavourably, but as Mr Peabody the assistant bank manager pointed out, men were better able to cope with somebody ready to use a knife than a woman. Gerald took his turn at watching, carried messages on his scooter, and seemed not to notice the jokes, some good natured and others less so, based on the fact that he was the only resident of the original Arcadia to join the committee.

'Think they're too good for us, I dare say,' Mr Frampton said. 'Don't want to join the *hoi polloi*.' He smiled as he said it, indicating how absurd it was to think a man like himself who drove a Roller (even though the firm's, not his own) could ever be classed among the *hoi polloi*.

The police viewed the Guardians' activities with tolerant amusement. Some hundreds of men convicted of various sexual misdemeanours had been turned up by their computer, and they were slowly eliminating them, but if the residents wanted to form this kind of vigilante committee – well, it could do no harm, and kept them occupied. But after several weeks, as there were no more attacks, and the nights grew colder, and there was a whole week when it rained every night, the Guardians' ardour faded. There had been some rather similar attacks twenty miles away, and it was agreed that the Guardians could be disbanded. 'We scared him off,' Mr Frampton said. 'He knew if he tried it again he'd get more than he bargained for.'

So, with mutual thanks and self-congratulation, the Guardians ceased to exist. But Gerald continued to walk round the executive houses of Arcadia with their wide pavements and large lawns, then round Greater Arcadia where the pavements were narrower, the lawns smaller and the houses much less individual, all of them having been built to one of four designs. He wore his woollen cap and the Guardian badge, and carried his father's cane, which had a large brass loaded top, in the shape of the dog-faced Egyptian god Anubis. Mr Burke had been amused by his son's insistence on acting as solitary watchman, and gave him the stick.

'It belonged to my father, and his father too. Give anybody a tap with the business end of it, and he'll know all about it.' He smacked the dog's head on to a cushion, and made a dent. Gerald nodded.

It was on a dark night in early November that Gerald caught the Soft Shoe Rapist.

His evening walk took a little less than an hour. He was halfway through Greater Arcadia when he heard the sounds of a window being thrown open, and a woman's cry. The lighting throughout the Arcadias was discreet, and it was a few moments before Gerald made out the house from which the cry had come, and then sensed rather than saw a figure moving down the drainpipe. He opened the house gate, ran across the lawn, and reached the figure just after it touched the ground. With a sweeping blow the figure knocked dog-faced Anubis out of his hand, but Gerald managed to catch hold of a leg, and the two bodies writhed together on the grass. A light showed in one of the houses and glinted on steel. Gerald groped for the knife. It disappeared, then he felt something push at his side, saw the knife raised again, now dark with blood. He felt no pain but the sight of blood made him angry; he put two great hands round the figure's neck and squeezed. There was another push at him, and another, then the figure was beneath him and his hands still round its neck, but the strength seemed to drain from them and they loosened. The figure lay beneath him, a gurgling sound coming from the throat. Then there were lights, lights everywhere, and voices. After that, nothing.

He woke in hospital several hours later, and learned that

he had been stabbed three times, once within a few inches of the heart. He had caught the Soft Shoe Rapist, who was escaping after another rape in which the victim had ignored his threat that if she did not remain silent he would come back and kill her. The rapist was a member of the Guardian Committee, Mr Peabody the assistant bank manager. He was not on the police computer.

Gerald recovered to find himself a national hero. The headlines ranged from ONE MAN GUARDS ARCADIA to UNARMED GERRY FACES KILLER RAPIST, with half a dozen variations in between. He gave several interviews from his hospital bed, and proved to be a natural headline maker. 'Gerry says it's Goodies versus Baddies,' one paper said. Another headed its story, 'The Simple Faith of the Man in the Woolly Hat,' and a third, ' "I Just Did What I Had To," Hero says'. The punning possibilities of his name were not ignored. 'Gerry Is No Berk' said Britain's best-selling tabloid, at the top of a story which began, 'Gerry Burke may look a bit of a berk in his woollen hat, but when it comes to defending law and order he's a tiger.'

After he came out of hospital Gerald was stopped in the street by people who shook his hand, and said it was young men like him, ready to go in there and take a chance, who were making Britain great again. He declined invitations to speak to local schools, Rotary Clubs and Chambers of Commerce, but appeared for three minutes on local TV, where in answer to a question about what he felt when tackling a man with a knife, he said, 'I didn't feel anything, I just did it, I knew he was a bad man and had to be stopped.' The messenger firm that employed him found he was in such demand that they doubled his wages.

To say Mr Burke was astonished by Gerald's sudden fame would be an understatement. Charles Cloudesley, a retired merchant banker who lived only three or four min-utes' walk away, embarrassed him by saying he had a hero for a son, and even his lord and master noticed one of the press stories, and said he was to be congratulated on having such a fine young man for his son. He felt like asking his lord and master if it was a matter for congratulation to have a son who was content to be an overgrown messenger boy, and read nothing but comics. He was irritated by Emerald, who said Gavin and his friends had been very impressed, and that she had always said he would be proud of Gerald if he gave the boy time.

The person who seemed least affected was Gerald himself. He went on reading comics and listening to pop records, and continued making his round of the two Arcadias at night, taking with him the loaded stick, which in reference to the dog-headed god who topped it, he called 'the dog'. 'I'm taking the dog for a walk,' he would say, looking at his father and step-mother to see if they laughed.

The dog was of service when, at the end of November, Gerald was patrolling (which was how he thought of it) Greater Arcadia, and saw a girl trying to get out of a car, and being stopped from doing so by a man inside. He was thirty yards away when he saw the car door open and the girl get out, then heard her scream as she was pulled back again. When he reached the car a struggle was taking place inside. He pulled open the door. The driver had his hands round the girl's throat, she was shrieking something and clawing at his face. When the door opened they both looked round.

They seemed astonished when Gerald shouted, 'Leave her alone.' The girl shrieked something at him, got out and pushed past. The man also got out of the car and came round towards her. Gerald barred the way. The man let out a volleyful of obscenities and hit Gerald on the jaw. Gerald brought the dog into action and gave the man a tremendous crack on the shin. The man collapsed to the ground. The girl jumped on to Gerald's back and pulled his hair, knocking off his woollen hat. He staggered, trying to shake her off, and inadvertently struck the car's side window with the dog. The tinkle of glass brought people out of nearby houses.

The encounter remained unreported in the press, perhaps fortunately. The couple proved to be man and wife, the man threatened to sue Gerald for assault, Gerald pointed out that he had struck the first blow. The matter ended with Gerald paying for the broken car window. He did not mention the incident to his father or to Emerald, but it became known, and he was transformed from a hero into something like a figure of fun. People at work asked if he had broken up any more happy families lately. Nevertheless, he continued to patrol Arcadia.

In December the weather became colder, the roads were icy, a little snow fell. Decorations appeared in windows, fairy lights on Christmas trees, circlets of holly round front doors. Gavin came home, bringing with him a girl student who seemed to view Gerald with the curiosity appropriate to a creature of another species. Both of them were bursting with high spirits and their gaiety infected Mr Burke, so that one night he joined with Emerald in a sentimental sing-song, with Gavin playing the piano. Gerald had no voice, and when he joined in the girl almost collapsed with laughter. At the office he was no longer in demand as a despatch rider, his fame seemed altogether forgotten.

In late December it began to snow in earnest, thick flakes that settled on the ground, and provided a carpet that silenced footsteps and made driving dangerous. A week before Christmas Gerald went out on what proved his last patrol. His faithful dog went with him.

He was still in Arcadia, the original Arcadia of big houses and discreetly dim street lighting, when he saw the man. Under the mantle of snow the individual outlines of houses were not easily distinguishable but Gerald was almost sure that it was the Cloudesley house from which the man emerged. The place itself was in darkness, and the man who came, not out of the front door but round the side of the house, was carrying a large bag over his shoulder. He made his way quickly yet stealthily to the gate, and hurried down the road.

Gerald quickened his own pace to catch up with the man, although this was not easy. There was nobody about, for they were in the midst of a really heavy snowfall. Snow blew into Gerald's face, blurring his vision, snow was wet on his mouth, and his wellingtons were more suited for trudging than hurrying. But still he gained ground, was near enough to call out. 'Stop,' he shouted, 'stop.' The man turned for a moment, long enough for Gerald to see that he appeared to have no proper face. Then he pulled a hood over his head and went on, more quickly than before. Gerald started to run.

He felt an exultant certainty that he had found a thief, a baddie, for if he was a goodie why did he not stop when hailed? Perhaps, with the baddie caught, that moment of fame would return.

He caught the man at the point where Arcadia ended and Greater Arcadia began, put a hand on his shoulder, swung him round. To his horror the stranger revealed not a face but a hideous mask. He put down the bag he carried, fumbled inside it. Before his hand could come out holding a knife or revolver, dog-headed Anubis struck. Raised high and then swung down like a mallet, he hit the stranger once, twice, three times. The man fell to his knees. The hood had fallen aside and the wig beneath it was askew, revealing a bald pate. He had been not only a thief, but one in disguise! Anger filled Gerald, anger and a wonderful aware-ness of his own rightness as he rained blows on that wickedly dishonest bald head until dog-headed Anubis was wet and dripping and the man lay still on the snow, his coat rucked up to show the red clothes beneath, his bag fallen open and a couple of the toys in it spilled out. The Santa Claus mask had slipped off too, revealing the face of old Mr Cloudesley.

The Inspector who took Gerald's statement had a sense of humour, and prided himself on being a bit of a wag.

'And you really thought he was – what did you call it? – a baddie.'

'Yes, I thought he was a baddie.'

'My, my. And it was just old Mr Cloudesley taking along a bag of presents to the Greater Arcadian Jumbo Christmas Gift Gala. He was going to be Santa Claus, you know.'

'I know it now, yes.'

'But you never recognized him?'

'It was the snow.' The Inspector's geniality was somehow more frightening than the long faces his father and Emerald had pulled when they came to see him. 'He should have stopped when I asked him.'

'And when he opened his bag to show you the toys for the kiddies, you thought—'

'He was going for his gun. Or his knife.' But Gerald only whispered the words.

Well, the Inspector thought, they say there's one born every minute, but they don't all go round thinking they're Wyatt Earp. Aloud he said, 'You know, you're going to be famous.' The young man's head was raised when he said that, the eyes sparkled for a moment, then dulled as the Inspector went on: 'You'll go down in history as the man who killed Santa Claus.'

Has Anybody Here Seen Me?

Out of the Underground train, along the platform, up the stairs, on to the escalator. Advertisements moving past, Best Pizza in London, it's mouthwateringly m-m-m-moreish, Michael Frayn play at Savoy, see-thru nightie that turns him on, Smirnoff the vodka, Morland's Can Find That Job You're Looking For, Dance All Night at the Fandango, Alligator Jeans Go Snap.

To the top, present ticket, up more stairs, out. Where?

Why, he thought, looking at the bookshop on one corner, Great Newport Street beside it, news-stand nearby, the theatre showing *He Did What She Wanted*, a new comedy, I know this place, of course I do. Then, seeing the Underground entrance saying 'Leicester Square', he shook with laughter. All I had to do was look at the station name as I came out, silly me. Leicester Square station, just round the corner the Hippodrome, then the Square itself. *Used* to be the Hippodrome, now Talk of the Town, something like that. I know where I am, of course I do. Couldn't recognize Leicester Square, did you ever? No I never, no I never did.

So here I am but the question remains, most unfortunately the question remains. Not where, but who? Face up to it, the name's gone. Who knows it, who's seen me, am I the invisible man? Familiar lines came into his head, he had to restrain himself from singing them:

53

> *Has anybody here seen me?*
> *M-e-double-e me,*
> *Where can me be?*
> *I left home at half-past ten,*
> *Haven't seen myself since then,*
> *Has anybody here seen me-e-double-e,*
> *me-e-double-e, me?*

A clever little song, but its entrance into memory was disturbing. Something wrong with it, something he didn't want to remember, something that made movement imperative. He said aloud, 'No use standing here,' bought an evening paper, crossed the road, walking in a businesslike manner as if he knew where he was going. He passed a shop that showed in the window brass doorknobs, door knockers, bathroom fittings, gilded mirrors. Stopped to consider his reflection in a mirror.

A tallish man, thin dark-blue jacket and trousers, mouse-coloured hair receding a little, smooth nearly delicate features, good figure, almost elegant really. Lines about the eyes though and, oh dear, as he looked more closely, some wrinkles in the delicate features. Age? Oh, say thirty-five – well, perhaps forty, no more than forty. Why should thought of age make alarm bells ring in his head?

And now that I've seen him: who is this stranger?

But *of course*, he mentally told the figure in the glass, there's really no problem in this case of lost identity. Just – it's so simple – just look at his wallet, credit cards, any stray envelopes bearing name and address that may be about his person. The figure in the glass felt its inner breast pocket. Nothing there. He watched with detachment as the figure, now a little agitated, felt in jacket, trouser, hip pockets, dredging up some five pounds in coins, and a shopping list made on a piece of paper evidently torn from a memo pad. Fillet steak, new potatoes, courgettes. Is that my writing?

The figure in the glass put the paper against the shop window to write on it, then checked himself. No pen.

Never mind, he told himself, no cause for alarm, I'm not lost, I know just where I am, could find my way without trouble around central London, no trouble at all, I assure you. All that's happened is a temporary black-out, happens to almost everybody at some time or another. A blockage, like that caused by wax in the ear. In ten minutes or perhaps less something in my head will go *click* as the ear goes *pop*, and I shall remember.

A drink might help.

Within a hundred yards a pub revealed itself. The sign outside showed two men staring at each other, one a respectable whiskered top-hatted Victorian, the other a jaunty crouching creature, half-man and half-ape, arms stretching well below his knees. The pub was called the Jekyll and Hyde. He pushed open the Saloon Bar door, went in.

'What'll it be?'

'A pint of best bitter.'

Did he know this pub, did he often drink bitter? The place was crowded, but he saw a vacant seat at one table, sat down, drank some bitter, gave an involuntary shudder.

The other man at the table was thickset, sandy, with a sharp enquiring nose. 'Great weather we're having. Can't have enough of it far as I'm concerned.' The words were said challengingly, in apparent fear of contradiction.

He realized that he was hot, uncomfortably so, shirt clinging to him. He nodded.

'The wife now, she don't like it. Get out in the garden, I say, enjoy the sun while you can, don't get much of it, this ain't California. Know what she says? Too much sun gives you skin cancer. I ask you, how many days do we get like this in a year, ten, twenty? Say thirty, the most I'll give you is thirty.' The glare seemed to call for a response, but he did not make it. 'All right, thirty. And that gives you skin cancer, I say to her, thirty days in the sun, is that what you're telling me? No good though, she covers herself up like she was wearing one of those Arab things.'

'Yashmaks.'

'Right you are.' The man looked at him with respect. 'You a regular? Seen you in here before, have I?'

'If you'll excuse me, there's something I want to read in the paper.' It was true, he had an overwhelming feeling that the evening paper contained vital information about his identity.

'Suit yourself.' The man picked up his empty glass, ordered a refill at the bar, took it to another table.

He opened the paper, an early edition. He could not have said what he expected to find, perhaps a name he would recognize, perhaps a picture of the man in the shop mirror. He turned the pages quickly, not reading but looking for a name, a picture, something he felt must be there.

Nothing. Now he went through the pages more slowly, lingering over the news stories. On the front page discussions about an atomic pact, and in a separate panel 'This Time the Wolf Kills'. The Wolf, it seemed, was a burglar and rapist who had terrorized an area in south London. He was uncannily skilful in entering houses through skylights, windows closed but not locked, basement areas. He cased houses carefully, making sure that only one person was there, and that a woman. Mostly they were married, and the Wolf struck in the late morning or early afternoon. He threatened the woman with a knife, raped her, then took any jewellery he could find. In this case the woman had resisted, there had been a struggle, the Wolf had stabbed her to death. Significant clues, the story said, were being followed up by police.

What else? Scandal in a Home for Young Delinquents, Big Drugs Haul at Heathrow, Pop Star Tells All, Arson Suspected in City Fire, Man in Spy Enquiry Vanishes.

'Civil Servant James Hetherington, recently interrogated in relation to the missing Ministry of Defence papers, left his home in Clapham yesterday morning, and has apparently disappeared. His wife Jennifer said he left just as usual after breakfast, taking his briefcase and saying he might be a little late that evening . . .'

'Is this seat taken?'

A woman stood beside his table, glass in hand, half-smiling. He said it was free, and she sat down. A young woman, thirty-five perhaps, unobtrusively dressed, gold ring on wedding finger. Was there something about her he recognized? Now she did laugh, raised her glass. 'Seen enough?'

'I beg your pardon. It's just that I thought . . .'

'Yes?'

'Do we know each other?'

She looked at him over the rim of the glass, a short drink, probably gin and something. 'Well. What do you think?'

'I think perhaps we've met before.'

'Tell me the old old story. I mean, I wouldn't call that a new approach, would you?' Her voice was artificially refined.

'It isn't an approach. It's simply that I can't remember . . .'

'Where it was we met? That one's as old as the hills too. Never mind, I'm Rosemary. What's your name?'

'John.'

She had noticed the pause before he said it. 'That's not very original either. Are you going to buy me one, John? Gin and French.'

As he went up to the bar and ordered the drink he wondered: do we really know each other or not? Can I tell her the truth? The barman seemed to look at him oddly. Perhaps they knew each other too, he was expecting to be greeted.

'Do we know each other?'

The barman had a toothbrush moustache, hair cut very short. 'How's that?'

'I've been in this pub before, thought I recognized you.'

'You looking for trouble?'

'Of course not. Why should you think so?'

'You stay your side of the counter, I'll stay mine, right?' The barman stuck his face forward, pores were visible in his broad cheeks. 'Or put it this way, I don't know you, you don't know me, let's keep it that way, right?'

Rosemary was reading his paper. 'I hope you don't mind.'

'Of course not.'

'You've spilt something, John, stepped in it too from the look of it. Cheers.' He looked down and saw two dark patches on his left trouser leg, one near the bottom, the other above the knee. Another patch, or stain, marked his left shoe.

'This Wolf, I don't know what things are coming to, you're not safe in your own home. What you been up to then, John?'

Confession seemed inevitable. 'I don't know.'

'How do you mean, don't know?'

'This is important.' He leaned across the table, grasped her hand, but she withdrew it. 'Do we know each other or not?'

She looked away. 'That's a funny question. It was you said we knew each other.'

'Please listen. I said my name was John, but I don't know if it is or not. I don't know what it is, I've lost my memory. I think I only lost it a little while ago.' He was conscious that the words must sound absurd, as he saw her looking from side to side as if in fear of attack. The overlay of refinement had gone from her voice when she spoke again.

'I'll tell you what I think, John, you're a bloody nutter.

I'm a working girl, I thought you meant business, it wasn't me who started this what's your name lark. I don't know what you're after, but whatever the game is, I'm not playing. I'm going out of that door now and if you come after me I swear I'll turn you in. Now you remember that, *John.*'

She left the pub, hips swaying. As the door closed after her the barman stopped polishing a glass, stared at him as it seemed accusingly. He shook his head as if the action might help to shake those lost bits of memory back into place. Instead it brought to the surface another line or two of that song:

> *I'm an actress on the stage*
> *And I should be all the rage*
> *But I'm always losing* some*thing.*

How did it go on? Da da *da*, da da *da*, then the last line of the verse, 'And now I've lost meself.' Very careless, John or whatever your name is, you'd better find yourself again.

He looked at the pub clock. Two-fifteen. As good a time as any other for discovering your identity. He folded the paper carefully, put it on the table, got up, left the pub.

A fine afternoon in London. Two-fifteen, by now two-sixteen. *I left home at half-past ten, Haven't seen myself since then.* Did I buy the fillet steak, if so where is it? Let's hope I didn't leave it out so that the cat could get at it. Do you own a cat then, John? Don't know.

Take the first right, second left, leads down to the river. Is that so, how do I know it? But I do. Down to the river, on to the bridge, vault the parapet, no problem it's quite low, then down down, an endless descent that lasts only seconds. The water, cold, dirty. Make no resistance. Finish.

That's what you may *think*, John, but things aren't that simple. Always a dozen busybodies around just waiting for people to jump off bridges, raise the alarm, strip off, jump in, life-savers to a man or woman. Man or woman created He them. But did He, is that so?

For that matter they say the moment you hit the water you struggle, don't want it, never meant things to end like this, swim with a nice easy crawl to safety. Never meant to enter that cold river, officer, just leaning over the parapet to look at my reflection, Narcissus complex you might say, leaned that tiny bit too far.

Stop it, stop it, he said to himself – or had the words been spoken aloud? He took the first right. A narrow street this, small shops, shabby, seems familiar. Newsagents, antique shop Victoria Regina, 'we sell all the rubbish Grandma threw out', barber's pole, heads bent over basins, attendant waves and smiles. At me? Go in, ask, Excuse me, who am I? Have you seen me? Has anybody here seen me? Drawn a blank, Oh dear, thank you kindly, sorry you've been troubled. But where can me be?

A couple of lines of patter: *I'm so forgetful, you know, last night I got home, took me clothes off and tucked 'em up in bed, then hung meself up in the wardrobe.* But let's be frank about it, this is no joke. *Has* anybody here seen me? Waiting, waiting for the click of recognition.

It did not come. He took the second left, and at once felt uneasily: I know this. On the left there will be an Italian restaurant named Ruggieri, a cut-price men's clothing shop, a block of flats named Atlas Court. And on the right? The right was boarded up. There were cracks in the posters and he crossed the road, looked through. A half-demolished building stood there, a sign in front of it: 'For All Demolition Work Come To D. E. Stroyer.' On the damaged façade of the building the word 'Theatre' remained, and on the walls below two or three torn placards. One showed the picture of a top-hatted monocled Victorian toff, and said 'Burlington Bertie Is One of the Boys', another was of a woman wearing an enormous picture hat, with 'Outrageous Olivia, Outré With Oomph' beneath.

'Good afternoon to you.'

He turned. A tramp perhaps, but if so a burly and upright one. Clothes old and shabby, trousers with old-fashioned turn-ups and slightly frayed at the bottom, but grey hair neatly brushed, and a waxed grey moustache giving an air somewhat military yet hardly genuine. The voice too had something assumed about it, rather as though it were being issued from a ventriloquist.

'Lookin' at the old place, then? Victim of the property developers, a damned shame. And what do they do with it? Two years now, and it still isn't even properly knocked down. Just sittin' on it, every month it's worth another few thou. A demned shame I say.'

'Perhaps you can remind me, what was it called?'

The man stared. 'Remind you? Ay should say so. Remind you of the Old Tyme Theatre, that's extremely droll.'

He gestured at what lay behind the boarding. 'I've forgotten exactly your connection, I'm afraid.'

The man pulled at his moustache, faintly clicked his heels. His voice took on momentarily the stentorian tones of a circus barker. 'Percy Cudmore at your service, formerly sar'n't major in Her Majesty's Indian Army, now employed to keep this rabble in order. Remember now, old man? Kind of combined commissionaire and chucker-out. Not that there was any need for the chuckin' out line, though some of the lads got a bit above themselves at times. *You* remember that, or should do.' His left eye closed in an unmistakable wink.

'I'm afraid not.'

'If you say so. No offence meant, none taken I hope.' He stood a little closer, garlic and beer discernible. 'Times are diff for an ex-sar'n't major, old man. Can't even get a job as a pub bouncer, say I'm too old and not up to it, can you believe it? The same not true of your good self I hope, you're lookin' remarkably well an' flourishin'. Wish I could say similar. If you happen to have a bit of foldin' money superfluous to present needs it'd be much appreciated.'

Here was somebody who knew him. What could be simpler than to say: I remember we were both associated with this theatre, but exactly what did I do there, who was I? But the words were literally unspeakable. He had a feeling of dread, his limbs trembled, his throat seemed choked so that he could hardly breathe. He opened his jacket, felt for the wallet that was not there, then buttoned it again hurriedly, aghast at what the opened jacket had shown. But Percy Cudmore seemed to have noticed nothing.

He felt in his pocket, found two of the golden coins, put them in the hand that almost surreptitiously received them, then took a step backwards to remove himself from the body so close to his own. Hand closed on coins, transferred them swiftly to pocket, encounter over. Hand sketched a near-salute, jeering rather than respectful, and the words too seemed jeering, though they were harmless enough.

'Left the old foldin' money at home, worried about gettin' mugged I dare say, very wise. Many thanks, old man. Do the same for you one day, I hope.' Now Percy Cudmore, done with him, walked up the road, fifty yards away turned into a pub.

Hand shaking, he unbuttoned the jacket again. The right side of his shirt was spotted and smeared with red, there were stains on the jacket lining. He buttoned it once more.

Now his actions became decisive. He walked down to the end of the road, crossed it. The river was there, as he had known it would be. He walked along beside it until he came to the bridge, but hardly glanced at the water. Left at the bridge, over the Thames. Now on the south side, he went through a minor maze of narrow streets without troubling to look at their names, steps unerring.

All this was a kind of sleepwalking. He had no idea of who he was, or what would be at the end of this apparently purposeful left-right, left-right. He no longer sought to find a name for himself. I am me, he thought, no need to look further. Has anybody here seen me? Never mind whether they have or not, whether I left home at half-past ten or not. If I did hang myself up in a wardrobe and put my clothes to bed, it's nobody's business but mine. The only person concerned is me-e-double-e, me-e-double-e, me.

Steady now, only a song. Don't take it seriously. Petrol station on corner. Turn right.

But, honestly, admit it. I'm always losing something, and now I've lost meself.

Do I wish to find me, him or it?

He turned another corner, stopped still. This was a mews, the street cobbled, garages on either side, little houses above them. The houses had been tarted up, newly painted blue, pink, white. Pot plants outside the front doors. At the far end a knot of people, two or three police cars. He made his way towards them over the cobbles, treading delicately as a cat. Faces turned towards him expectantly. He smiled, nodded. Yes, I know you. It is me, not you, that has disappeared.

A copper in uniform at the door looked enquiring, but feet clattered on the stairs, a man appeared. 'Chief Inspector Hawkins, just the man we're looking for, come on up.' He followed the chief inspector up the stairs into the living room, then put hand to mouth in dismay.

It was, or had been, a pretty room. The Italian china ornaments on walls and tables in the shapes of gloves, shoes, opened books, were a little chichi, the *trompe l'œil* window opening on a country scene with real curtains over it was rather preposterous, the tubular chairs and tables were out of key with the ornaments and the window, but still it had been a pretty room. Now most of the ornaments were smashed, the curtain had been pulled down, lighting fittings were broken. Glass and china littered the floor.

'Somebody went a bit berserk, wouldn't you say?'

Hawkins was rosy-faced, smiling, his manner jolly. 'But you ain't seen nothing yet.' He led the way along past a tidy kitchen to a bedroom. There was blood everywhere here. It had spurted over the walls, marked the white carpet, there were splotches of it on the pink sheets. He shook his head, he could not have said why.

'Looking for the body? Went half an hour ago, no need to worry. Now then, sir. Your name is Oliver Raynes, and you share this delightful residence with one Archibald Burton, now the late Archibald Burton, agreed? And the said Archie had recently been showing an undue interest in a young actor by the name of Leon Padici, agreed? And according to your next-door neighbour Archie had been communicating to you the idea that he'd prefer your room to your company as the old saying goes, he'd like you to move out and Leon to move in.

'And this same neighbour heard a most tremendous barney going on early this morning – couldn't help hearing, he says, the shouts and shrieks woke him up – as a conclusion to which Archie succumbed to attacks with a meat chopper from the kitchen, the assailant being apparently under the impression that Archie was a side of beef that needed carving. He then did the demolition job you've seen in the next room and exited into the street where the ever-watchful neighbour saw him. Or you.'

The words made no impact on him. He was staring at a poster on the wall which had escaped the general carnage, except for a spot or two of blood. It was one he had seen outside the theatre, showing the woman in the picture hat. It was signed: 'Dearest Archie, with all my love, Olivia.' The chief inspector was still talking.

'Now here you are, come back to save us the trouble of looking for you, which I must say is very helpful. And with marks that show just what a naughty boy you've been.' He wagged his round rosy head in reproof. 'I couldn't be sorrier, I'm one of your admirers.'

'Not me,' he said. 'It was not me. I could never have done such a thing. This is not me.' He took off his jacket, threw it on the ground, unzipped his trousers. 'Please. These are not mine. The clothes I wear are not me, nothing of all this is me. I am not me. Has anybody here seen me?' He looked wildly round, but the chief inspector was his only audience. His trousers dropped to the floor. Beneath them he wore frilly pants, lettered, 'Naughty But Nice'.

Hawkins laughed heartily. 'Your famous song, of course, *I left home at half-past ten, Haven't seen meself since then.* And very well you always delivered it. Pity the Old Tyme packed up. I used to enjoy those shows, took my old lady, we sang the choruses. Quite fancied you myself, as a matter of fact.' He laughed again, to show that this was a joke. 'And "I am not me", that sounds a promising line. It wasn't me hacked my friend to death, it was somebody else, please judge I wasn't there. Yes, very comical, I like it.' He restrained his amusement, as it seemed with difficulty. 'But now, Oliver Raynes, I must ask you to put these clothes on again. I am arresting you on the charge of murdering Archibald Burton, and must warn you that anything you say may be used in evidence. So come along, Oliver. Or should I say Olivia?'

The Birthmark

It is often said that doctors know of several undetectable poisons which they never mention in the presence of patients, but in truth these reports are much exaggerated, for they generally refer to beneficial medicines that may have a deadly effect if wrongly used. Insulin injections, for instance, are vital for diabetics but can cause death through hypoglycemia if injected into a perfectly healthy person. The truly undetectable poisons are discovered by research chemists, and the secrets of them remain buried in their laboratories. Or at least, that is where they should remain.

The use of such a poison was the undoing of Courtney Vance. After the trial and sentence, he freely admitted his guilt, complaining to prisoners and warders alike about his bad luck. 'It was perfect, really perfect,' he would say. 'Nothing could possibly go wrong.' Then he would launch into a lengthy account of the affair and just what did, unbelievably, go wrong. Courtney got a life sentence, which with remission generally means nine years in Britain, but he served only three of them. Another prisoner, who had slaughtered his wife and three children with an axe and suffered agonies of remorse ever since, was enraged by the endless repetition of the tale and Courtney's callousness about the crime. He stabbed Courtney fatally with a shiv made in the prison craft shop where they worked side by side. The axe murderer was sent to Broadmoor, where he in turn bored his doctors with an endless recital of grief about his lost family.

Courtney Vance was in his late thirties at the time of the murder, a senior sales representative for DPN Medical Supplies. The term 'salesman' was deprecated, but he was in fact a salesman and a very good one. His manner with the doctors and wholesale chemists on whom he called was confident but deferential, impressive both through his grasp of medical detail and his refusal to oversell any product. 'This is something that our wise men think may be helpful in certain arthritic cases,' he would say. 'But they do acknowledge it has limitations and, frankly, my own feeling is that there *may* be side effects in certain conditions, although of course I'm not a doctor.'

His smile conveyed, what was already known to many of his customers, that he might have been – could have been – a doctor if mysterious family troubles had not prevented him from taking the final examinations. In fact, he had failed his prelims twice, and then given up. Or rather his father, an assistant bank manager, had been told that it would be a waste of money for him to continue.

'They say you've got no application. "Not too bright and lacks application" – that was the story at school, and it's the same now. I don't know what you're fitted for, Bill, except to sweep the streets.'

Courtney said truthfully that it had been his father who wanted him to be a doctor, and he hoped it would not come to sweeping the streets. What did he feel inclined for? Some kind of journalism, perhaps – certainly something that wasn't tied down to regular hours in an office or a doctor's surgery. He had half a dozen jobs in as many years after giving up medicine, and left or failed at all of them before being taken on for a trial period by DPN. There he was a success from the start, and at the time of the murder had been with them for ten years. He worked from home, which was an outer suburb of London called Warners Green, although he was required to spend four weeks each year at the laboratories outside Northampton, where new products were tested, and another four at conferences where selling points were emphasized. He much enjoyed these occasions, when he impressed everybody by his authoritative manner, which was combined always with deference to superiors.

It was shortly after he got the DPN job that he married Evelyn Bridges, whom he had known at school. Her father was understood to be something influential in the City. Certainly he always wore a bowler hat when he drove up every day from Warners Green to town in his Mercedes – except on days when the Mercedes was to be seen outside the local golf club. His wife drove a small Lancia. 'They're a two-car family,' Mr Vance Senior said when his son told him he had been accepted by Evelyn. 'It's a good marriage, son.' His wife piped her eye and said it seemed like fate that they should have met again. Evelyn, like Courtney (who had by now discarded his first name of William, always detestably abbreviated to Bill), was an only child.

In fact, fate had received some assistance from Courtney. After that first chance renewal of acquaintance at a local Conservative Club dance, he had sensed that Evelyn was his for the taking, and had courted her assiduously. He was in his late twenties and had been thinking that it was time for marriage. This was even truer of Evelyn, who was a couple of years older, plump, placid, and plain. In a physical sense she was hardly a catch, but there was the Mercedes, the Lancia, that 'something in the City' aura of money. It was a church wedding, the reception for a hundred and fifty people was held at the best local hotel, Mr Bridges paid for a honeymoon in Paris. He waved aside Courtney's thanks. 'You're one of the family now, m'boy.'

Being one of the family, however, did not bring the benefits Courtney had hoped for, even expected. When Mr Bridges had a heart attack and died on the golf course a couple of years later, the bowler hat proved to have been, as one might say, a deception. Whatever Mr Bridges had been in the City, it was something not very important, or not very profitable. He had lived consistently above his income. The house had to be sold; the Mercedes went, of course; the Lancia was replaced by a Mini; the widow settled down in a small flat. For Courtney and Evelyn there was nothing at all.

It was true, as she said, that they had each other, and by now Courtney had received promotion at DPN. They lived in a neat little semi-detached house in a row of almost exactly similar houses, with a pocket-handkerchief garden in front and a bigger patch behind. There were in the first months no children, something which Evelyn regretted but which secretly pleased Courtney. He was a careful, cautious man and regarded a child as an expense they really could not afford. This was something Evelyn knew, as she seemed mysteriously to know everything about him. He realized the depth of her understanding when she suggested he should have a vasectomy.

'You know you don't want children,' she said. 'Admit it.'

He found that difficult. 'It isn't exactly that I don't want them – it's what they cost. I've worked it out, and the annual expense when you take everything into account—'

'It doesn't matter. I want us to be happy, Court, that's all.'

'I should like you just to look at these figures, they show the situation so clearly—'

Evelyn looked at the figures and said yes; he had the vasectomy, and felt distinctly relieved. They had quite a busy social life. The senior Vances and Mrs Bridges came round to Sunday lunch or supper at regular intervals, and both Courtney and Evelyn were pillars of the local Conservatives. There were socials and bazaars, at homes, tea and supper parties. Evelyn made little scones and cakes and homemade jams, and was an excellent housekeeper, working always within the agreed sum he gave her each month. 'She's a wonderful little wife, son,' the now retired Mr Vance Senior said after a supper party of beef olives, potatoes done in some French manner with cream or butter, and a green salad, all washed down with cheap but flavoursome supermarket wine. Courtney did not dissent, although 'little' was by now a misnomer, for Evelyn enjoyed her own cooking and was distinctly big.

It was because of her size, Courtney told himself, that he indulged in occasional peccadilloes. His success as a salesman for DPN products had led to an extension of his territory, so that he often spent a night or two away from home. On these occasions he looked deliberately for one-night stands, and often found them. These peccadilloes – which was the word he always used to himself about them – did not, he felt sure, affect his marriage. Even so, it was disconcerting to find that Evelyn's ability to understand him extended to them.

'Would you say you married me for my money, Court?' she asked one evening. That was ridiculous, he said, he hadn't had a penny from her family. 'Correction, I should have said in hope of making useful contacts, perhaps Daddy getting you into some glamorous job, and finally inheriting a nice little packet when he died.'

'If you put it that way – well, not exactly, but some of those thoughts might have been in my mind.'

'Still, it hasn't worked out badly, has it?' He kissed her and said it had been marvellous.

'No, marvellous isn't the word, but it's been all right. You're doing well, we have a lot of friends, I'm good at running the house—'

He interrupted her to say truthfully that she was a wonderful manager.

'Only trouble is, you don't like fat women. Don't interrupt, you know it's true. And I'm fat, can't be helped, something to do with metabolism, I've read it all up. You go on doing your duty, but I know it is a duty. Remember when you used to bring me flowers, give me scent? Not any more. And you're working off some of that surplus energy when you're away for the night. No need to worry about it. I just want you to know that I know, and don't mind, that's all.'

There was something uncomfortable about being so thoroughly understood, but he didn't deny what she had said. Instead, he asked how she could put up with him. She said, with a sparkle in her eye, 'Because you're just about the handsomest man I ever saw, that's why.'

At this time Courtney Vance was certainly handsome. In youth he had looked immature and uncertain, but success, confidence, and the passing years had greatly improved his appearance. He looked, he thought himself, like a film star in the days when they dressed well, bathed and shaved often, had hair that was properly brushed and combed – Cary Grant perhaps, with a touch of David Niven. An old-fashioned look. Well, he didn't pretend or wish to be one of your long-haired teenagers in jeans. His thick dark hair was becomingly flecked with grey at the sides, his figure as slim now as it had been when he married, his profile as clear-cut. There was a suggestion of weakness in the wobbly, shapeless mouth, and of self-satisfaction in the way he smoothed his little moustache, but taken all round Courtney Vance was undoubtedly a handsome man, and for many women an attractive one.

A day or two after that conversation, Courtney bought Evelyn flowers, and a week later a bottle of Magical Night, the tangy fragrance of which had enlivened their honeymoon. Evelyn smiled, thanked him, patted his cheek. He was pleased, but also a little resentful. Did one bring home a bottle of sexy perfume to be patted on the cheek like a child? But he enjoyed his job and admired his wife even though he did not love her passionately. If he had been asked whether he was a contented man he would have said yes.

Then, a year before the murder, he acquired a mistress.

Thelma was the American-born wife of a local building contractor named George Hartley, a great bull-necked man with a voice which seemed always to be issuing through a megaphone. Courtney had found himself sitting next to her at a Conservative Club dinner and they had got on wonderfully well from the start. Not surprisingly, perhaps, since almost her first words were: 'I've seen you at meetings often enough, and you know what I've always thought? One day I'm going to be sitting next to that man and then I'll say it straight out to him.'

'Say what?'

'Tell him he's the most attractive man in the room. There, I've said it.' Dark eyes flashed at him. 'I know Evelyn already, we're on a couple of committees together. She's a honey. But you've got no time for that sort of stuff, I know. Evelyn says you're a busy man.'

He told her what he did, implying that it was only a matter of time before he was invited to join the DPN board. 'And your husband is—?'

'Over at the next table. The man with the thickest neck in the room. And the thickest skin. He only thinks about one thing.' There was a pause before she said, 'Money. He's away a lot, too.' She turned and faced him directly. She had a high colour, strong features, flaring nostrils. The side of her face that had been turned away from him was marred by a birthmark, going from cheekbone to temple, purplish and menacing. A smile touched her lips, then she turned away abruptly and spoke to her neighbour on the other side. What had she been hinting?

He asked Evelyn about her, casually, tactfully, and learned that Hartley had met her at some convention where she was handling public relations for the English end of an American firm. They had been married within a few months, both for the second time.

'Some of the Tory ladies don't like her. Think she married George Hartley for his money, and that might be true – she's years younger than he is. Then she offers to do this and that, and they think she's pushy. If you ask me, they're just jealous. I like her. How old do you suppose she is – thirty?'

'I really hadn't thought.'

'She *is* very direct, says what she thinks. How did you get on?'

'Well enough. She's rather aggressive for my taste.'

'You like everything to run smoothly, no rows, I know that.' She smiled at him. It was true, but he slightly resented her knowing it, and saying so. Indeed he found himself more and more irritated by the way in which Evelyn seemed always to know what he thought in advance.

It has been said that Courtney Vance was a cautious man. He had no wish to do anything that might affect his marriage, his work, or what he thought of as his social position. All the peccadilloes had taken place well away from home, and although he thought about Thelma Hartley and the look she had given him, it was not until she came into the local pub where he was having lunch that he did anything about it. It would have been absurd not to eat their sandwiches and drink their beer together. He asked what she was doing there.

'When George is on a trip I can't be bothered to cook for one, often go to a pub. What about you? I thought you were always away.'

'Doing a round of local calls. I'm off on a little tour tomorrow – Surrey and Sussex. I'll be away two or three days.' She said he was lucky. He thought quickly. On the following day his calls would, or could, take him within a few miles of Warners Green. He asked if she would have dinner with him, naming a hotel near enough for her to drive to it, far enough away to make it unlikely that any Warners Green resident would be there.

She drained her beer and said, 'I thought you'd never ask.' The birthmark glowed a fiery red. In some curious way he found this flaw on her otherwise perfect skin attractive.

In the hotel on the following night, they did not eat dinner but went straight up to the room he had booked in the traditional name of Smith. Before the act and after it, Thelma talked. She said that she was bored with the bull, which was what she called her husband, bored with Warners Green, bored with the stuffiness and pettiness of local politics. Courtney said he was bored, too, although that was not true.

She walked out naked to the bathroom, showered, and came back. 'You've done this kind of thing before.'

'Not *this* kind of thing,' he said, and meant it. Her passion and eagerness was strange to him. Afterwards she had been dripping with sweat. He didn't ask about her own experiences, afraid of what he might hear. What followed was not exactly a night of bliss, for Courtney was nervous of such raw excitement as she displayed, but it was certainly a night of a kind outside his knowledge, one he wanted to repeat. At one moment she said, 'What about Evelyn? You going to tell her?'

He was shocked. 'Good heavens, no. Certainly not. You surely don't intend—'

'To tell the bull? No, he might fly off the handle, though let me tell you, he's no reason to complain. He's got a string of floozies. I've found letters in his pockets. If I wanted to, I could take George for half the money he's got.' Her mouth shut like a trap, her natural colour was heightened, the birthmark glowed.

Over the next months, there were a dozen occasions when she stayed at hotels with him. Sometimes Hartley was at home and she had to say no. Courtney then felt deeply frustrated, but he did not seek out other women in her absence. They had been peccadilloes – this was the real thing, a grand passion.

He was slightly embarrassed by the fact that Thelma and Evelyn became very friendly. Twice he came home from trips during which Thelma had spent a night with him to find her in the living room.

'She's really interesting,' Evelyn said. 'Got quite a different slant on things. Perhaps it's because she's American.'

'I shouldn't see too much of her if I were you.' He added rather feebly and absurdly that she had a doubtful reputation. He never had a real row with Evelyn – as she had said, he did not care for raised voices – but some acrimonious words passed and he brought her flowers on the following day. She accepted them with a smile and patted his cheek.

One night, at a hotel in Brighton, Thelma told him that she and George Hartley had parted. She laughed at his look of shocked surprise.

'Don't look so amazed, these things happen. No need to look worried, either – your name hasn't been mentioned. I told you I had the goods on George. It's separation by mutual consent, with what you might call a truly handsome settlement. He wants to marry one of the floozies after the divorce, which won't be yet a while. Do you know you've got the finest body of any man I've ever seen? Come here and let me make a spot check.'

A little later he said, 'You'll be leaving Warners Green.'

'Right. I've got my eye on a flat in Kensington.'

'That means the end for us.'

'I don't see why.'

But he knew it did. In Kensington, meeting again her sophisticated London friends, public relations people, and the like, she would soon forget him. He found the thought of life without her dismaying, and said so. Indeed, he used the word unbearable. She looked at him consideringly.

'We do seem to suit each other, don't we? Much better than most. Be a pity to lose it. But you'll come up to town and see me. And I'll still make little trips out to hotels. I quite enjoy the sordidness.'

They didn't have to lose it all, he said wildly – they could live together.

'What about Evelyn? I couldn't do that to her, break up her life. She's my friend.'

'I could talk to her, make her understand. She wouldn't want to stand in my way.'

'You're talking rubbish and you know it, Courtney Vance. For me you're a playmate, for Evelyn you're a husband. I don't even know that I like you, I just like what we do.' She took his hand and put it on the birthmark. 'And you might find that this put you off when you saw it every day.' He protested that he hardly noticed it. 'Mind you, you're such a pretty playmate that if Evelyn weren't there, I might want to have you for keeps. But she is.'

He knew that what she said was true, and went home dejected. Evelyn said, 'It's Thelma, isn't it? I shall miss her, too.'

'What do you mean?'

'I know about the two of you, of course I do. Oh, not from Thelma, she's said nothing. I knew what was going to happen when you asked those questions after the dinner.'

'But didn't you *mind*?'

'Oh, yes, I minded.' Her placid moon face, a double chin now distinctly visible, smiled at him. 'But it seemed to make you happy in ways I couldn't, so I put up with it. A lot of marriage consists of that, putting up with things.'

When Courtney paid his annual visit to the laboratories outside Northampton, Thelma was still living in Warners Green. She had moved out of her husband's pretentious neo-Gothic house, but the Kensington flat was still the subject of argument about the lease. Evelyn had suggested that she should move into their spare bedroom, but the idea shocked Courtney, and he rejected it out of hand. So Thelma was staying with a niece of her husband's, but she saw Evelyn almost every day.

On the drive up to Northampton, Courtney felt he was escaping from an awkward and slightly ridiculous situation. He had been altogether bowled over by Thelma, but could see no chance of a permanent relationship with her while Evelyn was there, and he quite accepted that Evelyn would always be there. The thought of Evelyn's death, and the possibility that he might cause it, never entered his mind. If he had ever considered such a thing he would have rejected the idea as far too dangerous. It might rather fancifully be said – and afterwards Courtney often and tediously said it – that Heinz Muller turned Courtney Vance into a murderer.

Heinz was an experimental research chemist, who was allowed to be a law unto himself within the firm. He was the chief of something called the Possibilities Ambit Laboratory, called Pal for short, where ideas derived from articles in scientific papers all over the world were tried out. Most of them never got beyond the testing stage, but every so often Heinz came up with a winner, something that could plausibly be called a variant on an existing product or technique, and was marketed successfully. He was unmarried, a Pickwickian little man with merry eyes behind gold-rimmed glasses, a hard drinker and inveterate womanizer. He and Courtney had got along well from the first time they met and had done some peccadilloing together.

On this visit, Courtney went as usual round the various labs, including Pal, talking to the scientists and technicians about what was in the pipeline. In Pal he was greeted warmly. Heinz showed him blends of this or that bubbling in retorts, rats and mice injected with various serums that made their behaviour depressed or manic, caused or were meant to cure skin infections and various diseases. At one end of the lab were little jars and bottles of possibilities promising enough for full-scale testing. Most would be found to have undesirable side effects, with luck one or two might be considered for marketing. Heinz talked about them all with enthusiasm, little eyes gleaming. Courtney knew enough to ask informed questions and he was genuinely interested. Heinz picked up two bottles, one large containing a cloudy liquid, the other small with liquid of a clear yellow colour. He held up the large bottle, which was labelled Noscan.

'*Very* promising, *quite* revolutionary, amazing. You know pregnant women now all have the maternity scan to see where the baby is positioned, and so on? But it can have bad effects if repeated, so some doctors say. You take Noscan, and you can forget the scan. After a dose of it, an X-ray plate shows everything as clear as if it were an etching.'

'What's the snag?'

Heinz looked comically offended. 'I do not say there is any snag. There is perhaps a little local difficulty – a matter of adjustment.'

'How do you mean? What's in the other bottle?' The small bottle was labelled simply NX.

Heinz chuckled. 'Pure poison.' He might have been Mr Pickwick enjoying a Christmas game at Dingley Dell. 'I read an article by a German scientist about the properties of the juice of the beloa shrub which grows in the Brazilian rain forests. The Indians there use it mixed with mud to heal wounds and sores, and they think it is magical, a cure for everything under the sun. I don't tell you how I get it, but this is pure beloa juice. No colour, no taste, but pure poison. You handle it with kid gloves, as they say. Spread a little on your handkerchief and inhale it, let a few drops go on the skin, and – phut, you're dead. No pain, no symptoms, no traces, just dead.' He laughed heartily.

'Then it's surely no use.'

'Ah, that is the local difficulty, the adjustment needed. It is the beloa juice that makes the etching, you understand. We have to find out how to counteract its poisonous effects, yet it must remain effective. We cannot be like the Indians and mix it with mud – it has to be a liquid. So we try different mixtures. This is Noscan 7, the seventh mixture. We tried the first six on mice, rabbits, guinea pigs.'

'With what effect?'

'They all died. That is our local difficulty. But enough of Noscan. Shall we see each other this evening? Go out on the town? I have arranged a little something.'

Heinz came round to Courtney's hotel after dinner. They had drinks and talked, then they met two of what Heinz called his professional amateurs, housewives ready to make a little extra money, but in the end Courtney declined the chance of a peccadillo, feeling a guilt about being unfaithful to Thelma which had never touched him in relation to Evelyn. Muller took one of the professional amateurs back to his apartment, but Courtney gave money to his and apologized for not being in the mood.

He spent a sleepless night. It was true he had accepted that Evelyn would always be there, but that was based on the belief that anything else was impossible. She had known about and tolerated the peccadilloes, known about and tolerated Thelma. What was it she had said? 'Marriage consists of putting up with things.' He saw years and years of toleration ahead, years in which she would get monstrously fat, plumping up like a giant cushion. And she would know always, as she seemed to, just what he was thinking and doing, and would put up with it. The prospect appalled him. And in the back of his mind there echoed those words of Thelma's: 'If Evelyn weren't there, I might want to have you for keeps.' He changed it mentally to *I'd long to have you for keeps.*

All this – he had to be honest with himself and admit it

– would never have come to the front of his mind but for
Heinz's talk about Noscan and the little bottle of NX. He
had asked one or two questions – casually, quite casually –
while they waited for the professional amateurs, and Heinz
had been delighted to expand on his discovery. The poison
worked by inhalation, by drinking, by contact with the skin.
It caused no pain (very important, Courtney thought – he
would never have considered anything painful), and left no
traces (equally important). Rabbits and guinea pigs just
keeled over, suffering heart failure (Evelyn was overweight).

Courtney thought and thought about it. He was a
cautious man, and if there had been the smallest possibility
of detection, he would never have considered the idea. But
there was no such possibility. If Heinz had exaggerated and
the whole thing failed, nobody would know.

The problem, then, was to get access to the bottle
without being seen by Heinz. But there again, he told
himself, if no opportunity arose he would take it as a sign
that he should leave the whole thing alone, have nothing to
do with it. None the less he prepared himself by buying a
tiny phial, a little pipette, and a pair of rubber gloves.

In the end, that particular problem was solved with
absurd ease, as if by destiny. He always stayed three days at
the laboratories, and on each day visited Pal to chat with
Heinz. On the last day, Heinz's assistant was on the next
floor searching some records in the library and Heinz was
called to the telephone, so that he was alone in the
laboratory. The little bottle was three-quarters full. He put
on the rubber gloves, poured no more than half an inch of
liquid into his phial, and stoppered it. The operation took
no more than a few seconds. He was pleased to see the total
steadiness of his hand.

After that, the car of destiny bore him onwards. If he
had any doubts about the need for action they were removed
when, on his return, he found Thelma installed in the spare
bedroom. The Kensington lease was still presenting prob-

lems, Thelma had had a row with the niece, Evelyn thought it only right that she should come and stay.

'After all, Thelma's almost one of the family,' Evelyn said in the placid unshockable way that succeeded in shocking, and even disgusting him. Thelma looked at him with sparkling dark eyes and seemed amused by his reaction. The limit came when, a couple of nights after his return, Evelyn said, 'If you want to go in to Thelma tonight, I shall understand.'

He was horrified. 'Certainly not. Under our roof, how can you suggest such a thing?'

'What does it matter whose roof you're under?'

He could not explain. The essence of his affair with Thelma was its romantic, exciting quality. To fornicate with another woman, with his wife's knowledge and compliance, in their own home – the idea was unthinkable. The suggestion removed any lingering doubt about the need for action, sealed Evelyn's fate.

Evelyn had used up her Magical Night. He bought another bottle, unscrewed it, and with the utmost care added the contents of his phial. When he gave it to her she thanked him, then said with her placid smile that they had had few magical nights lately.

He was going away on the following day and said with what he felt false heartiness that if she used it on the day he returned – or even before, if she felt inclined, in preparation as it were – they would see what they would see. He hoped that with this hint, the affair, which was the word he preferred to use, would be over before his return. It seemed wise to be absent. If Heinz should have been mistaken and the procedure was *not* painless, he feared he might be unduly distressed.

He was therefore not greatly surprised when, on the third evening of his four-day tour, he was told that Inspector Jezzard was in the hotel lobby and would like to see him. He was prepared to show shock and a touch of grief, the speech ready prepared. 'Good God, Inspector, I can hardly believe it. Evelyn seemed perfectly well when I left home, but of course – now that I think of it, she'd complained of what we both thought were indigestion pains.'

The speech, however, was never made. The Inspector, a sharp-eyed, sharp-nosed man accompanied by a sergeant, said, 'Mr Courtney Vance? I have a warrant for your arrest on the charge of wilful murder of one Thelma Hartley – hold up, man.'

Courtney Vance had fainted clean away.

His bewilderment was total. How could it conceivably have happened? At first he tried to fence with the Inspector, discover how much he knew. How was Courtney accused of administering this so-called poison?

'No point in playing games, Mr Vance. You know very well it was contained in a bottle of scent called Magical Night.'

'And you have been able to isolate the poison in the bottle?'

The Inspector smiled, not pleasantly. 'We know where it came from. We know you abstracted a certain amount of a highly toxic plant poison known as NX from your firm's laboratory and added it to the bottle of scent.'

'I don't accept that for a moment, but I ask again, have you been able to isolate the poison you say is in that bottle?' There was no reply. Heinz had been right, it was undetectable. 'If not, how can you be sure it was present?'

'In the most practical way. Very small quantities from the bottle have been added to food given to rats and mice. They died within half an hour. Painlessly, I understand.'

This was a shock. Perhaps he should have been present at the time, after all, to remove the bottle and pour away the contents. The Inspector continued. 'When we contacted your friend at the laboratory, Mr Muller, he confirmed that the effect was exactly that of this particular poison. He then checked the NX bottle and confirmed also that the level was lower than it should have been, although the fact had not previously been noticed.'

But why did you have any suspicion at all? he longed to ask. Instead he said, 'I admit I gave a bottle of Magical Night to my wife, Evelyn. I certainly didn't give one to Mrs Hartley.'

'It is not suggested that Mrs Hartley was the intended victim. That was your wife.'

'Then how—'

'Mrs Vance seems to have suspected some joke on your part, a cruel joke she said. According to her, you had an intimate relationship with Mrs Hartley. Do you wish to comment on that? It isn't important, since we have been able to check on some of the hotels where you stayed together. The bottle was meant for your wife. She gave it to Mrs Hartley, saying something to the effect that it had not secured any magical nights for her. Mrs Hartley laughed, opened the bottle, sniffed it, dabbed a little on her hand, then on her face. Within a few minutes she collapsed. In less than an hour she was dead.'

Had Evelyn suspected, had her uncanny understanding of him gone so far that she realized he meant to do her harm, and deliberately passed on the bottle?

'And then?'

'Your wife called a doctor. By the time he arrived, Mrs Hartley was dead, apparently from heart failure. The death would have been accepted as natural but for one remarkable thing. It was something your wife noticed. Once it had been pointed out, it was clear that something must be wrong and that further investigation was needed. We were called in, and took it from there.'

'*Yes?*' he said. '*Yes?* What was it?'

The Inspector smiled again. 'I think Mr Muller told you

not only how powerful NX was, but also of its remarkable properties?'

'He did, but what then? What was it Evelyn saw?'

'It was rather what she did not see. Mrs Hartley had a red birthmark on one side of her face. She had dabbed a few drops of scent near to it. What your wife noticed was that, within a minute or two of the liquid being applied, the birthmark had completely disappeared.'

Waiting for
Mr McGregor

Prelude

Even in these egalitarian English days nannies are still to be seen in Kensington Gardens, pushing ahead of them the four-wheeled vehicles that house the children of the rich. On a windy day in April a dozen perambulators were moving slowly in the direction of the Round Pond, most of them in pairs. The nannies all wore uniforms. Their charges were visible only as well-wrapped bundles, some of them waving gloved fists into the air.

The parade was watched by more people than usual. A blond young man sat on a bench reading a newspaper. A pretty girl at the other end of the bench looked idly into vacancy. A rough-looking character pushed a broom along a path in a desultory way. The next bench held a man in black jacket, striped trousers and bowler hat reading the *Financial Times*, a man of non-descript appearance with his mouth slightly open and a tramplike figure who was feeding pigeons with crumbs from a paper bag. Twenty yards away, another young man leaned against a lamppost.

A pram with a crest on its side approached the bench where the blond young man sat. The nanny wore a neat cap and a blue-striped uniform. Her baby could be seen moving about and a wail came from it, but its face was hidden by the pram hood. The pram approached the bench where the man in the black jacket sat.

The blond young man dropped his newspaper. The group moved into action. The young man and the girl, the three people at the next bench, the man beside the lamppost and the man pushing the broom took from their pockets masks which they fitted over their faces. The masks were of animals. The blond young man was a rabbit, the girl a pig, the others a squirrel, a rat, another pig, a cat and a frog.

The masks were fitted in a moment, and the animal seven converged upon the pram with the crest on its side. Half a dozen people nearby stood and gaped, and so did other nannies. Were they all rehearsing a scene for a film, with cameras hidden in the bushes? In any case, English reticence forbade interference, and they merely watched or turned away their heads. The nanny beside the pram uttered a well-bred muted scream and fled. The child in the pram cried lustily.

The blond young man was the first beside the pram, with the girl just after him. He pushed down the hood, pulled back the covers and recoiled at what he saw. The roaring baby in the pram was of the right age and looked of the right sex. There was just one thing wrong about the baby. It was coal black.

The young man looked at the baby disbelievingly for a moment, then shouted at the rest of them: 'It's a plant. Get away, fast.'

The words came distorted through the mask, but their sense was clear enough, and they followed accepted procedure scattering in three directions and tearing off the masks as they went. Pickup cars were waiting for them at different spots in the Bayswater Road, and they reached them without misadventure except for the tramp, who found himself confronted by an elderly man brandishing an umbrella.

'I saw what you were doing, sir. You were frightening that poor—'

The tramp swung a loaded cosh against the side of his head. The elderly man collapsed.

The baby went on roaring. The nanny came back to him. When he saw her he stopped roaring and began to chuckle.

Somebody blew a police whistle, much too late. The cars all got away without trouble.

'What happened?' asked the driver of the car containing the blond young man and the pretty girl.

'It was a plant,' he said angrily. 'A bloody plant.'

Trial and Verdict

Hilary Engels Mannering liked to say that his life had been ordered by his name. With a name like Hilary Mannering, how could one fail to be deeply aesthetic in nature? (How the syllables positively flowed off the tongue!) And Engels, the name insisted on by his mother because she had been reading Engels's account of conditions among the Manchester poor a day or two before his birth – if one was named Engels, wasn't one almost duty-bound to have revolutionary feelings? Others attributed the pattern of Hilary's adult life to his closeness to his mother and alienation from his father. Others said that an only child of such parents was bound to be odd. Others still talked about Charlie Ramsden.

Johnny Mannering, Hilary's father, was a cheerful extrovert, a wine merchant who played tennis well enough to get through the preliminary rounds at Wimbledon more than once, had a broken nose and a broken collarbone to show for his courage at rugby, and when rugby and tennis days were over became a scratch golfer. To say that Johnny was disappointed in his son would be an understatement. He tried to teach the boy how to hold a cricket bat, gave Hilary a tennis racquet for his tenth birthday and patted the ball over the net to him endlessly. Endlessly and uselessly. 'What I can't stand is that he doesn't even try,' Johnny said to his wife, Melissa. 'When the ball hit him on the leg today – a tennis ball, mind you – he started snivelling. He's what you've made him, a snivelling little milksop.'

Melissa took no notice of such remarks, and indeed hardly seemed to hear them. She had a kind of statuesque blank beauty which concealed a deep dissatisfaction with the comfortable life that moved between a manor house in Sussex and a large apartment in Kensington. She should have been – what should she have been? A rash romantic poet, a heroine of some lost revolution, an explorer in Africa, anything but what she was, the wife of a wealthy sporting English wine merchant. She gave to Hilary many moments of passionate affection to which he passionately responded, and days or even months of neglect.

In the nursery years which many psychologists think the most important of our lives, Hilary was cared for by big-bosomed Anna, who washed and bathed him, wiped his bottom when he was dirty, and read to him endlessly the stories of Beatrix Potter. Peter Rabbit, Squirrel Nutkin and Samuel Whiskers, Pigling Bland and Jeremy Fisher became figures more real to the small boy than his own parents. And brooding over all these nursery characters, rather as Hilary's father brooded with angry discontent over his unsatisfactory household, was the farmer Mr McGregor, who had put Peter Rabbit's father into a pie, and whose great foot could be seen in one illustration about to come down on Peter. Anna read and Hilary shivered, finding in the figure of the farmer an image of his own frightening father.

Childhood does not last for ever, but there are those who cling to childish things rather than putting them away. Hilary went up to Oxford – which to Johnny Mannering was still the only possible university – in the early sixties, just before the days of the Beatles and permissiveness. There he displayed the collected works of Beatrix Potter on his shelves beside books more fashionable for an undergraduate. 'But, my dear, these are the existential masterpieces of the century,' he said in his pleasant, although thin and slightly fluting, voice. 'The passions, the deceits, the *poignancy* of it all; really, Proust and Joyce are nothing to it.' Beatrix Potter gave him the only celebrity he achieved at Oxford. He joined two or three radical groups and left them within a few weeks, did a little acting but could not remember his lines, had three poems published in a small magazine.

He had just one friend, a broad-shouldered, blond, puzzled-looking rugger blue named Charlie Ramsden, who had been at Hilary's public school, and had always regarded him as a genius. This view was not changed when Hilary took as poor a degree as his own, something they both attributed to the malice of the examiners. Hilary, on his side, treated Charlie with the affectionate superiority one might give to a favourite dog. 'You must meet Charlie,' he would say to new acquaints. 'He's terribly good at *rugby football*.' Charlie would smile ruefully, rub his nose and say, ''Fraid I am.' They were really, as the acquaintances remarked with astonishment, almost inseparable. Not long after he came down, Hilary surprised his friends, not to mention his parents, by marrying a girl he had met in his last year at Oxford. Joyce was the daughter of an old and enormously rich family, and the wedding got a good deal of attention from gossip writers. Charlie Ramsden was best man.

The marriage was six months old when Johnny Mannering, driving home with Melissa after a party, skidded on an icy road and went over the central barrier into the lane of oncoming traffic, where his car was hit head-on by a lorry. Both Johnny and Melissa were killed immediately. At the age of twenty-five Hilary found himself the distinctly rich owner of the family business. Within another six months his marriage had ended. Hilary never told anybody what was in the note that Joyce left upon the drawing room mantelpiece of their house in Belgravia, beyond saying that she had done the boringly conventional thing as usual. There was no doubt, however, that she had gone away with a man, and his identity did cause surprise. The man was Charlie Ramsden.

Hilary divorced Joyce, she married Charlie, and they settled in South Africa, where he became a farmer. Those closest to Hilary (but nobody was very close to him) said that he recovered from the loss of Joyce, but that he never forgave Charlie Ramsden. He never mentioned either of them again. In the years that followed, he gathered the biggest collection of Beatrix Potter manuscripts, first editions and association copies in the world, put up money for a radical magazine, with which he became bored after a couple of issues, and for two plays, both of which were flops. He travelled abroad a good deal, sometimes in the company of young actors who appeared in the plays. In Amsterdam, on one of these trips, he met Klaus Dongen.

Klaus was half Dutch, half German, a revolutionary terrorist who believed that destruction of all existing national states must precede the advent of a free society. His group, the NLG or Netherlands Liberation Group, claimed credit for half a dozen assassinations, including one of a prominent Dutch politician, for a bomb that blew up in a crowded restaurant, and another in a shopping precinct that killed twenty people and injured twice that number. Klaus was not interested in Hilary's ideas but in his money. Hilary was not interested in Klaus so much as in his NLG associates, who seemed to him as fascinatingly dangerous as panthers, perfect associates for somebody named Hilary Engels Mannering. It was through Klaus that Hilary got in touch with young men and women of similar beliefs in Britain. He did not take them on trust. Each of them was required to perform an illegal act – arson, theft, violent robbery – before acceptance into the BPB. What did BPB stand for? The Beatrix Potter Brigade.

It was of course Hilary who had chosen the ludicrous name, and he had gone further, giving members of the group names of characters in the stories and insisting that they should wear appropriate masks when carrying out group exploits. Among their achievements were a bomb planted in a cabinet minister's house (it exploded, but unfortunately everybody was out), a fire bomb that had burned down most of a large London hotel, and a wages theft from London Airport. Hilary himself stayed in the background, interviewing possible new recruits and setting them tests which some refused to undertake. He would then explain that he was a theatrical producer who had been testing their reactions (which was true enough in a way), and pay them off with a ten-pound note. The enterprise had the elements of theatricality and childishness that he loved, and for three years now it had completely absorbed him.

On the afternoon of the unsuccessful attempt in Kensington Gardens, the members of the group gathered in an extension of Mannering's wine cellars that ran below the Thames near London Bridge. They entered by a door in an alley, which led to a passage and a storeroom. In the storeroom a perfectly camouflaged door led to a single large, windowless room. There were wine racks along two walls, with dusty bottles in them. On the other walls were prints of Beatrix Potter characters – the cat Simpkin buying food for the tailor of Gloucester, Mrs Tiggy-Winkle the hedgehog in her kitchen, Pigling Bland on the way to market, and of course Peter Rabbit, who was shown escaping from Farmer McGregor's attempt to catch him with a sieve. The ceiling was low and the lighting came from lamps invisibly sunk into it, so that the effect was one of mysterious gloom. There was only one visible door, which was said to lead directly to the Thames.

'It's romantic,' Klaus Dongen had said when he saw it. 'And ridiculous.'

'And safe,' Hilary had replied.

There were ten of them besides Hilary, and he waited until they all arrived, refusing to listen when both Peter Rabbit and Simpkin tried to tell him what had happened. Hilary was now in his late thirties, a tall, thin man with a sharp nose and a mouth perpetually turned down at the corners as though he had just tasted something bitter. He was older than the rest of them, and although his fluting voice had something absurd about it, he seemed in some indefinable way dangerous. His restlessness, his jerky movements, the sudden grimaces intended as laughs, all gave the impression that he was inhabited by some violent spirit which he was only just able to keep under control.

'Now that we are all here,' he said at last, 'I should like a report on what happened. Peter, you were in charge of the operation.'

The thick-set blond young man said, 'It was a plant; they must have been on to it the whole time. It's a bloody miracle we all got away.'

Hilary sighed gently. 'That is hardly the way to present a report, Peter—'

'My name's not Peter. I'm sick of playing kids' games.' There was a murmur of agreement. 'If you'd set this up properly—'

'Is that the way it goes? You're blaming me, yet you are incapable even of presenting a report on what went wrong.'

'How can you present a report on a disaster?' He stared down at the table as though he were a discontented schoolboy, and he looked remarkably like Charlie Ramsden.

Hilary pinched out the end of a Russian cigarette, used a long, narrow lighter and puffed blue smoke. 'Since you are unable or unwilling to present a report, I must do so myself.'

'You weren't there,' said the tramp who had been feeding pigeons.

'Really, Squirrel Nutkin? Would you like me to describe the man you hit when you got away?' The tramp looked at him unbelievingly. 'I was on the seventh floor of a building almost opposite, watching through binoculars.'

'But not present,' somebody said.

'Not present, as you say. The directing mind should be separate from the executive hand. But let us examine the affair from the beginning. It was suggested by a foreign colleague that we should take the son of the Duke of Milchester and hold him for ransom. The sum asked would be a quarter of a million pounds, which the Duke could comfortably have paid by selling a couple of pictures. Now let me tell you the object of this – to use a piece of deplorable American slang – snatch. Why do we want the money? It is to give financial backing for a project to be undertaken from overseas by a very, *very* famous person. Can you guess?'

'The Wolf.' The pretty girl who had sat on the bench with the blond young man breathed the words reverently. And reverence was in order. The Wolf was the most famous terrorist in the world, a man who killed with impersonal detachment, and had never been known to refuse a job if the fee was big enough.

'Well done, Pigwig.' Hilary smiled, but even his smile was acid. 'But it is not wise to use that name. I shall call him Mr McGregor, the ruler of all the little Flopsy Bunnies and squirrels and mice and pigs. And do you know Mr McGregor's target, his projected target?'

'One of the newspaper owners?' Squirrel Nutkin suggested.

'A politician? The Chancellor, the Prime Minister?' That was Pigwig.

Hilary shook his head. 'Look higher.'

'You don't mean—'

'Oh, but I do. Mr McGregor will be aiming at – what shall I call it – the highest in the land.'

There was a gasp around the table. Again Hilary gave them his acid smile. Then the blond young man said, 'But it all went wrong; we couldn't even get the kidnapping right. Why should the Wolf think we can set up an almost impossible job when we've fallen down on this one?'

'The Wolf – Mr McGregor – sets up his own jobs, as you call them. We should be his paymaster, nothing more. But as you say, this exercise went wrong. We had not one but two dress rehearsals, and you knew exactly what the nanny looked like. So what happened?'

'The baby wasn't the Duke's. It was pitch black.'

'That's right. I looked into the pram, I saw it.' Pigwig nodded agreement.

'They knew what we were doing and substituted the baby. And you can see what that means.' The thrust of his jaw, the jutting of his chin, were really very reminiscent of Charlie Ramsden.

Hilary rose, walked quickly and silently over to a cupboard above the wine racks and opened it to reveal glasses and, in a refrigerated section, several bottles of champagne. This was a ritual. When they assembled at the cellars there would always be champagne in the cupboard, and it was always Moët & Chandon of a good year. Pigwig, one of the group's newer members, had thought of saying that she would prefer whisky, but had decided against it.

The corks came out, the champagne was poured. Hilary raised his glass.

'I drink to Mr McGregor. And to the success of his mission. When he comes.'

'But he won't be coming now, will he? As you said, he only works for cash.' That was the man in the black jacket and striped trousers, an unnoticeable sandy fellow with a toothbrush moustache.

'Very true, Simpkin. But in the meantime we have a problem. The conclusion from what happened is simple and unmistakable.'

'Somebody grassed.' It was the only other woman round the table who spoke. She was in her late twenties, had a knife scar on her cheek and a heavy, ruthless face. It had been a touch of irony on Hilary's part to name her after the genial hedgehog Mrs Tiggy-Winkle.

'Again I deplore the use of slang, but it expresses a truth. Traitor, Judas, grass – it does not matter what name we use. The fact is that one of us must have told the authorities. Or told somebody else, who gave us away. Did any of you tell a friend, a lover, a wife, a husband?' Nobody spoke. 'Just so. It is as I feared.'

'There's one queer thing,' Simpkin said. 'If the counter-espionage boys were tipped off, why weren't they all over the place, why let us get away? Isn't it possible that it was a genuine change of plan, and we were just unlucky?'

'With a *black* baby, Simpkin? I should like to think that was true, but a black baby! Somebody was playing a joke on us.'

'I know who it was,' Peter Rabbit said. He pointed across the table at Simpkin. 'You.'

'And how does Peter Rabbit make that out?' There was an undercurrent of mockery in Hilary's voice, but he did not fail to notice that Simpkin was left sitting at one end of the table, the others drawing away as though he had an infectious disease. Simpkin himself seemed unaffected. He drained the glass in front of him, and refilled it from one of the bottles on the table.

'I'll tell you how I know,' Peter Rabbit began in a low, furious voice. Hilary stopped him. His eyes were bright with pleasure.

'We must do this according to law. There was no trial in any Beatrix Potter story—'

'Sod the Beatrix Potter stories,' said the man who had been leaning against the lamppost, a youth whose spottiness was partly hidden by his thick beard.

'Now then, Samuel Whiskers, no bad language *if* you please,' Hilary said indulgently.

The young man who had been pushing a broom spoke.

He was another recent recruit, a broad-shouldered figure with a round ruddy face and a snoutish, vertical-nostrilled nose which had led Hilary to christen him Pigling Bland. Like all of them except Peter Rabbit and Hilary himself, he spoke in the mid-Atlantic accent that denies the existence of English class distinctions.

'He's right. We don't want any playing about. If there's a grass, we've got to know who it is.'

'Precisely, Pigling. But let us do it by considering evidence rather than simple accusation. Simpkin, you are the accused; you may remain where you are. Peter Rabbit, you will be prosecutor; you should go to the other side of the table. The rest of you will serve as the jury and should group yourselves at the end. Thank you. I will serve as judge, summing up the evidence, although the verdict will be yours. I think I should sit away from you. Over here, perhaps.' He placed his chair beside the door. 'If you wish, Simpkin, you may ask one of the jury to defend you.'

'I'll defend myself,' Simpkin said. Of all the people in the room, he seemed the least moved.

'Very well. Prosecuting counsel, begin.'

The blond young man did not look at Hilary. 'I should like to say that this is a stupid way—'

Hilary tapped on the arm of his chair with the lighter he was using for another cigarette. 'Out of order. Produce your evidence.'

'All right. Simpkin joined the group four months ago. Since then he's been concerned in three jobs. The first was leaving a bomb in an Underground train. He did that himself. At least he says so, but the bomb never went off. Did he ever leave it?'

Simpkin intervened. 'Can I answer that?'

'Not now. You'll have your turn.' Hilary's eyes had been closed, and now he shut them again. With eyes closed, Peter Rabbit's voice sounded exactly like Charlie Ramsden's.

'Two. Simpkin was one of the people who planned to

get a comrade out of Brixton Prison. Almost at the last minute the comrade was moved to Parkhurst. Coincidence? Perhaps. Three. A couple of weeks ago, we should have had an open-and-shut job, getting documents out of a ministry file. They'd have been very useful to us. You, Jeremy Fisher' – he nodded at a man who had been driving one of the getaway cars – 'I don't know your name, so I have to call you that – you set it up; you had a friend on the inside. Simpkin is supposed to know the ministry layout, which is why he was involved so closely. The job went through all right, but the papers weren't in the file.

'And four, the job today. You were the grass.'

He stopped. Hilary opened his eyes. 'Is that all?'

'No. But I'd like to hear what he has to say.'

Simpkin's features were watchful; he really did look a little like the cat he was supposed to represent. 'No need to say much. One, I left the bomb. The mechanism was faulty; it was reported in the press.'

'Of course. You fixed a cover story.'

Simpkin shrugged. 'Number two was a coincidence, must have been. Number three, maybe the papers had been taken out months earlier. Anyway, why pick on me; why not Jeremy Fisher?'

'He wasn't in on the other jobs. You were.'

'So were you.' Simpkin permitted himself a brief catlike smile. 'And if you remember, I was against this snatch. I thought it was too risky.'

'I'm an old member, not a new one. We've made mistakes before, but it's since you joined us that things have been going wrong persistently. And of course you'd be against the snatch; that was another bit of cover.'

Hilary moved in his chair. 'You said there was something more.'

'Yes. Some of you know that I have – that I see people—'

'We know about your social position,' Mrs Tiggy-Winkle

said in her harsh voice. 'We know you meet the best people. I've seen your name in the papers.'

'All right,' Peter Rabbit said. 'Through my position I've been able to get a good deal of information. You know that,' he said to Hilary, who nodded and smiled his acid smile. 'Last Wednesday I had dinner at Horton's, which is a small luncheon and dining club with a very restricted membership. Top people in the services and the ministries, a few members of the government and so on.'

'Top people, period,' Mrs Tiggy-Winkle said. 'Nice company you keep.'

The young man ignored her. 'Horton's has a couple of rooms where you can take people for dinner if you've got something extremely private to discuss. On this night – it was fairly late, very few people in the club – three people came out of one of these rooms. One was Giles Ravelin, who's an assistant head in MI6. He's a member of Horton's, and the others must have been his guests. One was Sir Llewellyn Scott, who acts as a sort of link man between the police and the counter-espionage agencies. And the third was Simpkin.' He paused. 'I want him to explain how he came to be there. If he can.'

It was for such moments as these that Hilary lived, moments of excitement outside the routine of life. Revolutionary intrigue he had found for the most part boring, a matter of dull little men discussing how to obtain power over other dull little men. But the possible visit of the Wolf, the fun of calling him Mr McGregor, the tension in this long, low windowless room with its hidden light that made every face look ghostly pale – oh, these were the moments that made life worth living, whatever their outcome. How would Simpkin react to Charlie Ramsden – no, to Peter Rabbit? What would he say?

The silence was total. All of them were staring at Simpkin, waiting for Simpkin. At last he gave a faint, catlike cough. 'What was the light like?'

'The *light*?' Then he realized the question's purpose. 'A good deal better than it is here. Good enough to recognize you.'

'How near were you to this man?'

'I was four feet away or less, sitting in an alcove. You didn't see me, or I don't think so, because I was partly hidden. But I had a good view of you.'

'You saw the man for how long? Two seconds?'

'Long enough. It was you. I'll ask you again. What were you doing there; who do you work for?'

From the rest of them, those appointed as a jury, there came a murmur, an angry dangerous sound. 'Answer him,' Samuel Whiskers said. 'If you don't, we'll know what to think.'

'I can't answer,' Simpkin said flatly. 'I wasn't there.' There was a moment's pause while they digested this. 'I was never inside that place in my life, never heard of it. I gave him a chance to say he was mistaken, but he didn't take it. He's lying.'

The two men looked at each other across the table. 'You bloody Judas, you won't get out of it like that,' Peter Rabbit said.

Hilary steepled his fingers and offered a judge's comment. 'It comes to this, then: that we have an accusation but no proof.'

'You said it was last Wednesday. What time did this meeting take place?' the pretty girl known as Pigwig asked.

'Between ten and ten-thirty at night.'

'You're sure it was Wednesday, certain that was the day?'

As Peter Rabbit said he was sure, Simpkin seemed suddenly to wake from a brown study and showed his first sign of emotion, almost shouting at her to keep out of this, it wasn't her affair. She disregarded him.

'Last Wednesday, Bill—'

'You are not to use personal names,' Hilary cried. 'Pseudonyms *must* be preserved.'

'What stupid game are you playing; who do you think you're kidding?' she screamed at him. 'Half of us know who the others are and what they do, and those who don't could easily find out. At ten o'clock last Wednesday Bill wasn't at any Horton's Club or whatever it's called. He was in bed with me, had been all evening. Around eight I got up and made scrambled eggs, then we went back to bed.'

'Is that true?' Hilary asked Simpkin, who shrugged and then nodded. 'Two different stories. They can't both be right.'

The round-faced young man called Pigling Bland said, 'No, they can't. And I know who's telling the truth. A couple of days ago, I saw him – Peter Rabbit – walking along Piccadilly. He was with somebody who looked familiar, though I couldn't place him. But I knew who it was as soon as I heard his name today, because I've seen his picture in the papers often enough. It was this Scott, Llewellyn Scott.'

'You're sure?'

'I can't prove it, can I? But yes, I'm sure.'

'Does anybody else wish to speak? Very well. You have heard the evidence, and I don't think there's any need for a judicial summing up. Members of the jury, will those of you who find Simpkin guilty put up your hands.' No hand was raised. 'Simpkin, you are acquitted.'

'That's not the end of it,' Mrs Tiggy-Winkle said. 'He's the grass.' She pointed at Peter Rabbit, who seemed suddenly as isolated as Simpkin had been.

'He was lying. He must be the grass – stands to reason.' That was Samuel Whiskers.

'Do you wish to pass a verdict on Peter Rabbit?'

'I certainly do. Guilty.' Mrs Tiggy-Winkle's face was grim. The scar on it pulsed red.

'How many of you agree with her? Put up your hands.' They all went up except Simpkin's. 'Simpkin?'

'I just think he made a mistake. No need to suppose anything else.'

'Then who do you think grassed on us?' Samuel Whiskers shouted. Simpkin gave one of his characteristic shrugs.

'Peter Rabbit, you have been found guilty without a single dissentient vote. Have you anything to say?'

The blond young man passed a hand through his hair in a gesture intolerably reminiscent of Charlie Ramsden, and cried out in bewilderment. 'I don't know what's happening. This is all crazy, Hilary. You know me. You know it is.'

'No names, Peter. You know the rules,' Hilary said gently. He got up from his chair, walked over to the young man, held out his pack of Russian cigarettes. 'Let's talk about it.'

'I'll smoke my own.' Peter Rabbit shook one from a pack, put it in his mouth.

'Here's a light.' Flame shot up from the long, narrow lighter, and smoke came from the cigarette. Peter Rabbit looked at Hilary in total astonishment. He put a hand to his neck. The cigarette fell out of his mouth. He dropped to the floor.

Simpkin stood up. Somebody gave a cry, sharply cut off. Hilary giggled and held up the lighter.

'I got it from one of the NLG Boys. An ordinary lighter; you've seen me using it. But if you press a button at the bottom a dart comes out.' He pressed it and a tiny thing, hardly thicker than a needle, buried itself in Peter Rabbit's body in the wall poster. 'Very effective.'

'Nobody said kill him,' Samuel Whiskers said.

'The verdict was yours. There was only one possible sentence.'

'But he'd been in the group as long as me, as long as any of us.'

'There are no medals for long service.' Hilary gave his acid smile. 'This door leads to a chute that will deposit

Peter Rabbit in the Thames. If one of you will give me a hand, we can dispose of our grass. Then I suggest that we sit down and consider some new plans for raising the necessary cash to bring Mr McGregor over here.'

Simpkin helped him out with the body. They stood together while it slid down the chute and vanished. When they returned, an obituary on Peter Rabbit was pronounced by Mrs Tiggy-Winkle.

'Good riddance to bad rubbish,' she said.

Epilogue

Just after three o'clock on the following afternoon, Simpkin, whose name was Bill Gray, entered an office block in Shaftesbury Avenue, took the lift up to the third floor and went through a frosted-glass door lettered *Inter-European Holidays, Travel Consultants*. He nodded to the girl in reception and walked down a corridor to a room at the end. There, in a small office with three telephones in it, including one with a direct line to Giles Ravelin, he found Jean Conybeare and Derek Johnson – alias Pigwig and Pigling Bland – waiting for him.

'My God, what a shambles,' Derek said.

'Macabre.' Jean shivered. 'He enjoyed it, that Hilary Mannering. He's a real creep.'

'It was a bad scene,' Derek went on. 'If it hadn't been for Jean here, I don't know what might have happened. "He was in bed with me, had been all evening,"' he said falsetto. 'Wonderful.'

'You provided the clincher, Derek, with that story about meeting him in the street.'

Derek Johnson shook his head. 'Poor bloody Peter Rabbit – it was a clincher for him, all right. It was just his bad luck, Bill, that he saw you coming out of that room with Ravelin and Scott.'

Bill Gray was at his desk looking through papers about Operation Wolfhunt. Now he looked up. 'No need for tears. He was just an upper-class twit who got himself mixed up with a gang of thugs.'

'Mannering isn't a thug, he's a psychopath,' Jean said. 'The *pleasure* he took in using that lighter! I hate to be in the same room with him.' She asked curiously, 'Did you know he'd seen you at Horton's?'

'I was afraid he might have done.'

'So what would you have done if I'd not come up with that story?'

'Shot it out. But that would have wrecked the operation.'

'Mannering should be in a padded cell.'

'No argument. But let me remind you that if we take in his crackpot Beatrix Potter Group, we lose a chance of catching the Wolf. That's the object of the operation, remember? Now, we couldn't let them get away with kidnapping a duke's son, though I was able to make sure everybody got clear. They still have to raise funds to get the Wolf over here, and we've got to help.'

They waited. Bill Gray's catlike features were intent; he might have been about to pounce. 'I think this is going to come best from you, Derek. You've got a friend who's a watchman in a bank in Cheapside. He'll provide duplicate keys. There's wads of money in the vaults; we knock out the watchman and pay him off, collect the cash. The money will be slush, but they won't need to use much of it until they pay out the Wolf, and I'll put the word around so that in the meantime anything they use will be honoured. We'll talk about the details, Derek, after I've set it up. Then you can go to Mannering and talk about it. The Wolf's said to be in the Argentine at the moment, but he's in touch with an NLG man there and we have some contacts with him. When he knows that his fee's going to be paid, he'll come over.'

'And until then?'

A smile touched Bill Gray's face and was gone like winter sunshine. 'Until then we're waiting for Mr McGregor.'

The Conjuring Trick

A love affair may be like a conjuring trick. It is not always what it seems to be.

From the beginning, Robert Banister opposed the move to Marlborough Court from the house in Quinton Close. There was much more space in the house, he said, a garden at the back in which to sit out on sunny evenings, friendly neighbours. It was a community. To this Barbara responded that there was no comparison between the house and the apartment. If you lived in Quinton Close you stamped yourself as suburban and second-rate. Marlborough Court was in the city centre, an address that would impress people, a place where Robert could invite one of the Multiplex directors to dinner without the humiliation of having to explain where they lived and how to get there.

She added a clincher: 'We might get on better.' It was true that they snapped at each other, were annoyed by trivialities, seemed to have little in common. They had been married four years, and after the first had occupied separate beds.

So they moved to Marlborough Court, an E-shaped block of luxury flats, with a restaurant, an indoor swimming pool, and, of course, a porter and caretaker. Three apartments were vacant, but Barbara particularly liked one on the

107

sixth floor that faced inwards. It had a balcony with a delicate, though rather flimsy, wrought-iron railing. It was protected from the wind, and so would be just as good as Quinton Close for sitting out on sunny evenings. There was a living room with a sliding door opening on to the balcony, their bedroom, a kitchen with a breakfast bar, and a bathroom in which all the fitments were gold-plated. And that was all. The space was less than half of that in Quinton Close and it cost twice as much. When Robert pointed this out, Barbara replied that he was unable to recognize anything first class when he saw it. Within a week they were bickering as much as ever.

'It's like living in a rabbit hutch.'

'With less than half the work for me, do you ever think of that?'

'I was stuck for twenty minutes in traffic this morning, getting to the office. From the house there were never any traffic jams.'

'But if we wanted to go to the cinema, what then? I remember driving round and round to find a parking space. Now we can walk.'

Such squabbling can be affectionate, but theirs had an unpleasant edge to it, as if each was trying to put the other down. In fact, they rarely went to the cinema, and didn't watch much television. In the evening, Robert listened to classical music – Brahms, Beethoven, and Mahler, in particular. Barbara was a member of a bridge club and spent two or three evenings a week there. Sometimes Robert brought work home with him. He was an accountant at Multiplex, a firm with subsidiaries that sold everything from biscuits to bicycles. He had hoped at one time to become *the* accountant, but he was in his mid-thirties and further promotion seemed unlikely. Barbara was a few years younger and worked as a dental hygienist. Without her income, they could not have afforded to buy the lease of the Marlborough Court apartment. There were no children, because Barbara had said decisively that they could not afford them.

Robert didn't argue about it. Sometimes now he wondered why they had got married, although there had seemed nothing strange about it at the time. He had recently moved from a smaller firm to Multiplex at a considerable increase in salary, and he was tired of living alone and doing his own cooking. He had had a half-hearted affair with a secretary at the smaller firm and was relieved rather than upset when she told him she was going to marry one of the salesmen. Shortly afterwards, he had met Barbara on a visit to the dentist, where she had cleaned his teeth and said he looked after them beautifully.

As she bent over him, masked face within inches of his own, body slightly pressed against his as her powerful hands scraped at tartar, vaguely erotic feelings stirred in him. Her features, the hygienic mask removed, were strong and regular, thick brows almost met across her forehead, her chin was strong where his was indeterminate. She wasn't beautiful, but might have been called handsome. Everything about her was powerful in a way that impressed him, especially those strong managing hands. He pretended to an interest in bridge, she feigned a liking for concerts, and within a few weeks they were married.

Robert's parents had died when he was young and he was an only child – Barbara had been abandoned by hers and brought up by foster parents appointed by the local council. They had a brief honeymoon in the south of France, bought the house in Quinton Close, and settled to a kind of domesticity. But Barbara didn't much like cooking and Robert was not good at talking to the neighbours who came occasionally to dinner, and such occasions almost ceased after the first year. Barbara kept the house scrupulously clean and painfully tidy, Robert bought and planted annuals in the tiny garden. But that, too, was over now they were in Marlborough Court.

Robert couldn't have said what he expected from marriage, and so was not disappointed. When he looked in the glass he saw a tall, gangling man with regular features slightly flawed by the indeterminate chin, a trim figure in no need of dieting, small, well-kept hands. He had never taken too much to drink, never looked at another woman after his marriage. If he had been asked whether he was happy, he would hardly have known how to answer, for he never asked himself such questions, any more than he took any interest in which political party governed the country, although he felt it a duty to vote at elections. Nor did it occur to him to wonder whether Barbara was happy, or to concern himself that at night they stayed in their separate beds. He was aware that they didn't get on as well as they had in the first year, but then perhaps that was the way with all married couples. He realized she had some desire for a different, more luxurious or wealthier life and so didn't seriously resist the move from house to apartment, although he didn't like it.

Two weeks after they moved to Marlborough Court, he saw Lucille.

It was early evening. He was alone in the apartment because this was one of Barbara's bridge-club days, and he had taken a chair on to the balcony and was sipping the first of the two whisky-and-sodas he allowed himself after work while reading the evening paper. He glanced up from it, and saw a girl standing in the opposite window, naked from the waist up.

She had long, fair, almost golden hair, small beautiful breasts, and a look of childish innocence as she stared intently at something down in the street far below. As he watched, she stretched her arms upwards slowly, stroked one shoulder reflectively with the other hand, momentarily caressed a breast, smiled. Then she saw him and, still with the smile lingering on her lips, stepped back and out of sight.

His first reaction was to retreat from the balcony and close the sliding window. He felt ashamed of intruding on the girl's privacy, was aware of having relished the sight of that stretched arm moving lovingly over the shoulder and the hand lingering on the breast. He was also aware of feeling emotions Barbara had never aroused. She had impressed him by the self-confidence that he knew he lacked, but this girl looked frail, vulnerable, yet in movement and manner sensual.

He couldn't have said just when he began to try to work out what apartment she occupied and who she might be. His apartment, Number 65, was on a prong of an inner side of the E, he had looked sideways to the right when seeing her, so the girl's apartment, or that of her parents, must be next door. He opened the door, looked across the thick dark-blue Wilton landing carpet, and saw 64 in gold numbers. She must be behind that door.

When Barbara returned, he asked if she knew the name of their neighbours and she said she had no idea, adding surprise that he was interested.

He was disturbed to find that the vision of the girl remained with him, distracting him from some dull but complicated calculations about the financial position of a small company Multiplex thought of acquiring. He found himself looking out for her in the lift, and asked the porter the name of the occupants of Number 64, saying he thought he had recognized one of them as an acquaintance.

'That'd be Mr Delaporte. Can't be him, though – he's away on business.'

Robert mumbled that he must have been mistaken, the name was not Delaporte. The porter, young and curly-haired, looked at him a little oddly, and he realized he could have seen the name on the entry phone outside the entrance.

He saw her again a little less than a week later. He was coming back from the office and saw her at the entrance, carrying a bag containing several parcels. She put it down to open the entrance door and two small parcels spilled on to the pavement. He picked them up. She thanked him, speaking in slightly accented English. They got into the lift together, and at the sixth floor he realized he still had hold of the parcels. At her door she hesitated, then said, 'Please come in.'

They were in a large hall and passage, with several doors leading off it, then in a sitting room much larger than the Banisters', with several pictures on the walls. He had the parcels in his arms.

'Put them – oh, we will put them in Pierre's study, he is away.'

She led the way to a room as big as their bedroom, with a desk, easy chairs, more pictures. Robert had known theirs was one of the smaller apartments, but as he looked at the striped sofa in the sitting room, the elaborate flower arrangement, the pieces of china displayed in alcoves – Dresden or Meissen, perhaps, but obviously valuable – he realized fully that life in Marlborough Court was something to which he and Barbara should not have aspired. He should have said so, have said it firmly,

But now the girl was telling him to sit down, offering a cigarette, asking if he would like a drink. He said something about being her neighbour.

'I know. You saw me the other day.' He was overwhelmed with confusion, said he was sorry. 'Why should you be? I am stupid, I think here I am high up, nobody can see, but of course it isn't so. Anyway, what does it matter? My name is Lucille Delaporte. Chin chin.' She had poured him a whisky-and-soda, now raised her glass, and they drank together. He asked, half question and half statement, if her father was away. She laughed.

'Pierre is away, yes, but he is not my father, he is my husband.'

That made him more confused. He didn't know what to say, although looking at her now more closely, hair piled on top of her head instead of hanging loose, he realized she was not a girl but a young woman, although an impression of childishness and physical frailty remained. He remembered the sight of those girlish breasts, felt embarrassed, looked away, and saw in a corner of the room a brass-legged table with chessmen laid out on top. She followed his gaze.

'You like to play chess? I play with Pierre, but he beats me, he is so good.' They went over to look at it. He picked up two of the chessmen, and saw that they were real ivory and ebony.

'You will like to have a game sometime? But I tell you, I am not good. Perhaps you play Pierre when he comes back. He travels a lot. He is in France now or perhaps in Germany – he deals in art and also in jewellery. He has a gallery here – the Deux Arts, do you know it?' He had seen the gallery, which was in the city's most fashionable street. 'He travels to buy and sell things. He has a gallery also in Cologne, he says that is the great European centre for art. We have an apartment there in Cologne, but I like it here, except when he is away it is a little boring. I sometimes travel with him, but' – she shrugged – 'he is always so busy, and I have nothing to do.'

He finished his drink and said he must go. She came to the door and said now he knew who she was and where she lived, they were neighbours, perhaps one day they could have a game of chess.

He didn't mention the meeting to Barbara. To do so, he told himself, would have meant talking about the evident wealth of the Delaportes and saying how foolish they were to have come to Marlborough Court. That was no good, they were stuck with it now and could afford it – just. But he found himself looking at Barbara's scowling handsomeness, comparing it with Lucille's delicacy and fragility, and remembering that glimpse of her half naked. He longed to see her again but was too shy to telephone, or knock on the door of Number 64. One day he went into the Deux Arts Gallery, and was astonished by the prices asked for pictures which seemed to him mostly splodges of paint laid on very thick in vivid colours. The supercilious young man who gave him the price list said they were a new school of Latin American painters coming into fashion. The gallery also had a collection of modern jewellery, French and Italian, and again the prices seemed to him immense.

Ten days elapsed. He had been working late at the office. When he got home Barbara said, 'The people next door telephoned and asked us for dinner tomorrow. She said she'd met you. You never told me.' She barely listened to his explanation and seemed more interested in the fact that both the Delaportes had undergone teeth scraping at her hands.

Pierre Delaporte was a surprise to Robert. He was very small, a little smiling man who wore gold-rimmed spectacles hanging on a chain. He lifted these spectacles to look at things and people, perched them on his nose, then dropped them again so that they hung on his chest. The surprise was his age. Although lively in his movements, he was obviously between fifty and sixty years old, while Lucille could be no more than twenty-five.

They drank champagne and Pierre talked about his latest trip, which had taken him to five European countries. 'I bought only three paintings. That was in Copenhagen, a young Danish artist, he is going to be important. Lucille tells me you play chess. She says also you are very kind, you carry her parcels. We have a game one day, what do you say?' Robert said he'd like that, and agreed to come in for a game at the weekend. 'My Lucille, she is beautiful but she does not have a chess brain.' He pulled Lucille to him and held her close while kissing her lips, cheek, neck.

Barbara watched, cold-eyed. When they were back home she said, 'What a disgusting little man, slobbering over his wife.' Robert said he was exuberant. 'Is that what you call it?'

He asked what she thought of the apartment, and she replied that it was very fancy. 'They have lots of money,' he said. 'He has another flat in Cologne.'

'She told you that, did she?' Her dark intense gaze was bent on him. 'I could see the way she looked at you.'

Had she looked at him in a particular way? The idea had not occurred to him, and he found it attractive.

When he went round to play chess, Lucille watched them for a little, then sat on a sofa with her legs curled under her, reading a book, went on to the balcony, poured drinks for them, returned to the sofa. He was disturbed by her presence when for a moment she stood near to him, and distracted by it even when she was on the sofa.

Delaporte made his moves quickly, not always with much thought. After an hour, he threw up his hands in surrender, let the little gold glasses drop to his chest. 'You are too good, my friend – tonight, at least. You give me my revenge another time. But it will have to wait – we fly to New York next Wednesday.'

He said inanely to Lucille that she was going, too, and she screwed up her face. 'Pierre says I must, he wants me. I do not like the city, it is so noisy, so busy.'

'I give a little party there, my wife must be my hostess, that is her place, her job,' Pierre said, laughing. Still laughing, he put out finger and thumb and pulled at the lobe of her ear – as, Robert remembered, Napoleon had tweaked the ears of his favourite soldiers. Her reaction was not that of Napoleon's young men. She cried out that he was hurting her and ran out of the room. Pierre shook his head. 'Women, they like to live well, wear nice clothes, spend money. Sometimes they must be reminded they have duties.'

They had drinks, ate bits of things in pastry cases. Lucille was lively, even flirtatious. Pierre laughed and joked, yet there seemed to Robert something odd in their relationship, a passion that remained unexpressed.

He tried to explain what he felt to Barbara, who said he was imagining things. He also mentioned the prices of the pictures and jewellery at the Deux Arts, and that was perhaps what prompted her to remember the star cufflinks. They were gold links with tiny rubies and diamonds inlaid in the shape of a star, the only heirloom that had come to him from his father. He thought them rather showy and wore them only on occasions like the twice-yearly office dinner dance. She suggested he should ask Pierre how much they were worth, and was irritated when he said he would never sell them.

'Suppose they're worth a lot of money, two or three times as much as you expect?' she said. 'Anyway, I'm not saying we should sell them, only find out how much they're worth.' He shook his head. 'You're so feeble. Don't you see it might be a way of getting to know them better, they're the kind of people who might be helpful.'

'How?'

'How do I know? It was to meet people like them that we came here, wasn't it?'

'I thought we came here because we might get on better. That doesn't seem to be happening.'

She stared at him, then said she was sorry.

That night, for the first time in weeks, she came to his bed.

When he learned from the curly-haired porter that the Delaportes had returned from their trip, he telephoned.

Lucille answered, and said Pierre had gone away again for a couple of days, but, yes, she would love to come in for a drink.

She came, exclaimed at the prettiness of this and the cleverness of that in their living room, went out to the balcony and said the view was nicer than that from their apartment that looked the other way (a quick glance at Robert when she said that, a reminder of what he had seen). New York was always exciting and Pierre had done some business, but really she did not like it. She spoke mostly to Robert, as if she knew he would be a sympathetic listener, and Barbara said little, sitting with her heavy brows drawn together in a frown. He was surprised when she produced the little red morocco box containing the cufflinks and opened it.

Lucille exclaimed with pleasure and said she had seen nothing like them. He found himself tongue-tied, and it was Barbara who asked if Pierre would say what he thought they might be worth.

'Of course, he will be pleased. You would like him to make an offer for them?'

Robert broke in before Barbara could speak, to say no, all they wanted was that he should value them, so that they would know their worth for insurance purposes.

When Lucille had gone, he asked why Barbara hadn't spoken to him before showing the links. She glared at him and said she knew if it had been left to him he would have done nothing about it. They nagged at each other for half an hour.

In bed that night he compared Barbara with Lucille and wondered why he had married her. At breakfast next morning they hardly spoke. It was a relief to get to the office and bury himself in work.

The call came in the afternoon. When he lifted the telephone and heard Lucille's voice, he could hardly believe it. Nor had he heard her like this, obviously distressed, the words jumbled together, foreign accent pronounced, as she said she must see him. What about? She could not say on the telephone, but she must see him.

He rang the bell and she opened the door, her face anguished, took him into the big room with its china, ornaments, and pictures, and held out to him with a dramatic gesture the morocco box. He opened it and saw one cufflink. He stared at her.

'What happened?'

'I do not know.' Her hands were clasped tightly together. 'I take them out, look at them, they are so pretty – not pretty, beautiful. I put them on the dressing table. Then I am trying on clothes, I put on a shirt with holes so you can use buttons or links, I put your links in them to try. They are charming. I come in here, do this, do that, then I see one is not there any more. I am so sorry, so very sorry.' She began to cry.

It is not easy to cry without looking ugly, but she seemed to him just as beautiful crying as smiling. She also looked, as when he had first seen her, no more than sixteen years old. He put an arm round her, no more than that, and told her not to worry, it must be somewhere, they would look together and find it.

They searched the apartment, searched it thoroughly. They didn't find the cufflink.

When they were in the bedroom, both kneeling, looking under the bed, she began to giggle. It *was* funny, he saw that, two adults crawling over a bedroom floor looking for a cufflink. He began to laugh, too. Naturally – as it seemed, inevitably – she came into his arms, her face smudged with tears.

It was the first time he had been unfaithful to Barbara – which was the word he used to himself when he was back in their own little apartment and waiting for her to return. He felt ashamed. The most shameful thing was that he wanted to do it again, that when Lucille said she could see him tomorrow he had said yes. And that seemed possible, for next day was Wednesday, one of Barbara's bridge days.

The telephone call to him at the office on the following morning was hardly more than a whisper down the line, a whisper in which she said again she must see him.

'You've found it?'

She seemed not to hear the question, but asked him to meet her at lunchtime at the entrance to the Royal Arcade, which contained several of the city's most expensive shops. When he got there, she stood waiting. He asked again if she had found the cufflink. She shook her head, her expression that of a mischievous child.

'Then what are we doing here?'

She answered with another question. 'You have what they call a boiled shirt?'

'A dress shirt, yes, but why do you ask?'

She took his hand, led him into the Arcade, entered a shop that had in the window only a rope of pearls, a diamond pendant, and an emerald necklace, all unpriced. Inside, a man in frock coat and wing collar bowed, smiled, laid reverentially on a bed of black velvet three dress studs. In each of them a diamond glittered.

'What do you think? You like?'

He said they were beautiful, and before he could go on to the reasons why he could not accept them she had nodded to the frock coat, he was putting them into a little red box that looked identical to the one that held his cufflinks, she was saying they could be charged to Mrs Delaporte, and they were out of the shop.

'I have been careless, I lose something, I could not find cufflinks so I give a little present. There is no more to be said.' That was her reply to his stumbling objections, and when he tried to pursue them she said, 'Please, you must take them. If you don't, I shall not forgive myself.'

119

What happened after that again seemed inevitable. The curly-haired porter saw them as they walked through the entrance hall together and got into the lift. When it stopped at the sixth floor, Robert went without question into that grand apartment and there made love. He got back to the office very late, and it seemed to him that his secretary looked at him strangely. He found it impossible to concentrate on work, told her he had a bad headache, and left early.

He put the diamond studs into a drawer that he kept locked, and when Barbara came home she found him lying on the bed, staring at the ceiling. He told her he felt ill, and in a way that was true. The images of their love-making rose up before him and were played over and over in his mind, a tape endlessly repeated. He was repelled by what he had done, yet longed to see Lucille again.

For three days, he heard nothing from her. Returning home on another evening before Barbara, he stood out on the balcony for several minutes, as if by doing so he could rewind the tape back to the beginning, the vision of the golden-haired girl looking down into the street. But the French windows of the Delaporte apartment remained closed. Each morning and evening, going to and from the office, he looked at the blue door with its gold number, unsuccessfully willing it to open.

After those three days, he could bear it no longer and rang her from the office. There was a moment of silence when she heard him, then she said brightly, 'Hello, how are you? Did you want to speak to Pierre? He is here.' Then Delaporte was on the line saying something about his revenge at chess, and also that Lucille had complained of boredom, they were having a small party in a week's time and hoped he and Barbara would come. Robert said they would be delighted and put down the telephone with a feeling of overwhelming relief. Why had it not occurred to him that Pierre might have come home?

120

Who would be at the party? Should they after all go to it? Robert had a sudden feeling of revulsion, mixed with an unidentifiable fear. He had no particular wish to see Pierre again or to meet Pierre's friends. His only interest was in Lucille. And the fear, what did that come from? Perhaps from worry that the Delaportes' friends would be immensely sophisticated and talk about things in a way that left him looking and sounding foolish. Barbara became angry when he said something of this. Her eyes sparkled with a blend of indignation and contempt. She repeated those remarks about meeting people who might be helpful and said she didn't want to work for a dentist all her life.

So they went, and Robert soon saw that he need not have worried about being overawed. The other guests were a curious mixture, including the supercilious young man from the Deux Arts and a couple of other faces he recognized as residents of Marlborough Court. But there was also a girl with yellow and green hair that stood up in spikes and another who wore a halter and shorts that showed her navel, a Chinese wearing what looked like battle fatigues, a red-haired, loud-voiced American and his equally noisy wife, and a couple of swarthy little men who talked mostly to each other. Waiters from the restaurant brought around things on toast and smoked salmon done up in rolls. Robert spoke to one of the little men, who said his name was Arminias and asked if Robert did business with Pierre. He laughed when he heard that Robert lived in the next apartment, and laughed again as he said he was a business associate.

'You deal in pictures?'

Arminias laughed again. 'I am a picture framer, I choose the frame, prepare the picture. I am an important man. My friend Julio, he is important, too.' He indicated the other little man.

At that moment, Pierre came over, took Arminias away, and spoke earnestly to him, perhaps rebuking him for levity. Soon afterward, Arminias spoke to Julio and they both left. Barbara was talking to the girl with spiky hair. And Lucille? She had greeted him with a smile and a handshake when they arrived, but since then had not spoken to him, hardly looked at him. Yet what did he expect?

Delaporte asked if he was enjoying himself, clapped him on the shoulder before he could reply, and said they would play chess next week. Robert joined a couple on the balcony he recognized as local residents and learned that the man was the managing director of a building firm, and had recently bought a picture from Pierre. What did Robert do? The managing director's interest diminished when he learned that Robert was no more than an accountant at Multiplex. He half turned his back and began to talk to somebody else. Would that be turning a cold shoulder, Robert wondered as he re-entered the room. Most of the guests had left – it was time they, too, were gone. He tried to catch Barbara's eye, but failed. The girl with the spikes had her full attention.

Now the red-haired American and his wife were going, and Pierre left the room with them, the three deep in conversation, and Lucille came over smiling, two wine glasses in her hand. She gave him one, raised hers, and said, 'Chin, chin.'

He drank, and had time to remark that the drink was not his usual whisky before she took him by the hand. Then they were in the bedroom, still holding the glasses. She drained hers, gestured to him to do the same, and he did so. She took the glass from him, put it on a table, then was in his arms, shrugging off her dress, pulling at his clothes, urging him toward the bed. He tried to protest, to say this was madness, but she was murmuring something about Pierre being out for a while and they had time, and he gave way to her, gave way completely, pulling her down on the bed with an urgency equal to her own.

Now things were spinning and wheeling, he wasn't sure of place or time but was aware of himself as a different, more powerful person, so that when he felt a hand on his shoulder, rolled over and away from Lucille and saw Pierre's face purplish with anger and, as it seemed, enlarged, he was not alarmed but inclined to laugh. He was conscious of Pierre hitting him, and although the blows for some reason did not hurt he knew they should be resisted, and his strength was as the strength of ten as he got hold of Pierre and shook him to try to bring the little man to his senses.

After that, everything became out of proportion – the size of the room expanded so that the door seemed immensely distant, then as he crawled toward it along the carpet (he was on all fours, he couldn't bother to work out why) wall and door suddenly bulked up before him.

He hit his head on the wall and said, 'Knock knock,' hoping others would enjoy the joke. All the while there was sound, cries that seemed to come from a distance, Lucille's face alarmed and Barbara's frowning, unintelligible words coming from her. Then there was a need for air, the window and balcony a long way away, a day's crawl perhaps, but supposing you didn't run but leapt like a kangaroo, how long then?

Out of the door, along an endless passage, somebody was calling out his name and then there was a thud, a kangaroo kick at the back of his head. Unfair, he thought. It was the last thing he remembered from that scene . . .

What followed was a long nightmare, from which he constantly expected to wake and find himself in his office at Multiplex, papers round him, calculator on the desk, telephones to hand, secretary within call. But that vision was of a past reality. In the nightmare there were endless interrogations by polite, wooden-faced policemen. Then came conversations with an equally wooden-faced and equally polite solicitor who was acting for him and kept saying they must get his story straight, even though he repeatedly said he had no story.

There was a cell and then the prison hospital – there were all sorts of tests that involved metal bands put round his head and rubber ones round his arms. There was a series of talks with a pleasant, smiling psychiatrist who seemed to think there was no such thing as sanity, everybody was aberrant in one way or another. 'What has all this to do with me?' he asked. 'I'm simply an ordinary businessman who went to a party, was given an odd drink, and have no recollection of what happened afterward.' He corrected himself. 'I remember Pierre hitting me, and I shook him because he was so angry – I was trying to make him calm down.'

'You shook him? You don't remember a fight or a struggle? In the bedroom? Or later in the living room?'

'I only shook him. That was in the bedroom.'

The psychiatrist smiled, and made notes.

Everything was explained by his solicitor, and by Barbara, who came twice to see him and said she was doing her best. But what they said made no sense, he didn't remember the things he was supposed to have done. He listened with wonder as he sat in the dock while the prosecuting counsel, a man as urbanely pleasant as the psychiatrist, unfolded what he said was the story of a commonplace adulterous love affair that was not connected with the police investigation of Pierre Delaporte.

'You will hear police evidence that Delaporte had a perfectly genuine business as a fine art dealer, which he used as cover for smuggling drugs into and out of this country, and that his fine art business was not only a cover but positively a means of smuggling the drugs, which were hidden in hollowed-out cavities in the specially made picture frames. The police were aware of Delaporte's activities, but delayed making arrests at the request of their European colleagues. I understand many of these arrests have now been made.

'It was necessary that you should know this background because it explains the presence of drugs at the party where Delaporte died, but I must now tell you that his drug-running activities had no connection with his death. It is the prosecution's case that this is a simple matter of infatuation between an impressionable man and a beautiful young woman whose husband was away a good deal of the time. The infatuation was, as you will hear, on both sides. It was a short, stormy love affair that had a fatal ending.'

That fatal ending was described by the police witnesses who had found Pierre Delaporte's body on the ground eighty feet below the balcony from which he had fallen or been pushed. The flimsy balcony rail was badly twisted, presumably by the pressure of a body. Delaporte had been dead when the ambulance arrived, and beside him was a diamond-and-ruby cufflink which had presumably fallen from the dead man's hand.

Among the parade of witnesses that followed were faces barely remembered by Robert, faces that seemed to belong to another life. Here was the girl with yellow and green hair to say Pierre Delaporte had been her supplier for drugs, and that some people had taken them at the party. And there was one of the waiters who had seen Lucille and Robert go into the bedroom. When Mr Delaporte returned, he had looked for his wife, entered the bedroom, there had been shouts and screams. The waiter had gone in.

'What did you see?'

'First Mr Delaporte was punching Mr Banister. Then I don't know what you'd say – Mr Banister seemed to go crazy, he got hold of Mr Delaporte by the throat like he was trying to strangle him. I tried to pull him off and couldn't, so I hit him on the head with some big brass ornament I picked up and he just kind of collapsed on the floor. Mr

Delaporte, he was gasping for breath and then feeling his neck. He said something about settling this here and now and she said—'

' "She" being Mrs Delaporte?'

'Right. Mrs Delaporte, she said if they were going to quarrel there was no need for everybody to know about it, and Delaporte went into the living room – he was still feeling his throat and his face was a funny colour – and said the party was over. There were only three or four guests still there, and they left straight away. So then Johnny, the other waiter, and me, we started to clear up, but he said we should leave it and get out. So we did.'

'When you left, only Mr and Mrs Delaporte and Mr and Mrs Banister remained?'

'Right. Mr Delaporte was still feeling his neck and wiping his face. The two ladies, they were standing in the middle of the living room.'

'And Mr Banister? Was he still in the bedroom?'

'No – just as I left, he came into the living room. Didn't do or say anything, just stood.'

'What was your impression of him?'

'I'd say he was stoned out of his mind.'

That was the waiter, Frank. Then there was the curly-haired porter, to tell them that Mr Banister had asked who lived in Number 64 and that he had come in with Mrs Delaporte, laughing and joking. There was the frock-coated wing-collared salesman to speak of the purchase of the diamond dress studs, which proved to have been extremely expensive.

And then came Lucille. There was an appreciative murmur in court when she stepped into the witness box, wearing a plain black dress with a white collar, looking very young, frail, and beautiful. The prosecuting counsel led her through her story with almost old-world gallantry, dropping his voice a little at what might be thought delicate moments.

Yes, Lucille said, she had known Pierre Delaporte for

only six weeks before they married, and that was just two years ago. She knew only that he was a respected art dealer, nothing of any drug-running, although they smoked pot together sometimes, and she had once tried cocaine. And yes, it had been a happy marriage, Pierre was so dynamic – except that she did not like travelling and so usually stayed in England, which she loved. But at times she was a little lonely.

Up to this point she had spoken clearly, but she lowered her head and at times became barely audible as she told how she had met her neighbour Robert Banister and found him so charming, so considerate, all the things Pierre was not.

'I loved Pierre, but Robert was so different.' She lifted her head now and said defiantly, 'So English.'

'You became his mistress.'

The reply was whispered. 'Yes.'

She went on to tell the story of the lost diamond-and-ruby cufflink. 'I was so devastated, so ashamed I am so careless. I feel I must make it up somehow. So we go together to this shop, I give him these studs. It is a way of saying sorry to my lover, that is all.'

'This was a valuable present.'

She shrugged.

'You were buying something for your lover with your husband's money, did that occur to you?'

Her head lowered again, Lucille muttered, 'I did not think. It was very wrong, but I did not think.'

And then Pierre had found the missing cufflink, in the bedroom, under her dressing table. He had questioned her about it. He was angry and did not believe her when she said it must have been dropped by one of the cleaners and was of no value. He could see it was valuable. This had happened an hour before the party, and so at the party she had thought she would not talk to Robert, but when Pierre had taken some guests out to say goodbye she had brought over his glass, just to say hello. Robert had said he must talk to her alone, they had gone into the bedroom, he had kissed her and started to make love, then Pierre had come in, had been furious, they fought—

'Was Robert Banister his normal self at this time?'

She shook her head violently. 'Not at all. He was so strange – I had never seen him like that. I thought he would choke Pierre to death.'

'And then the waiter knocked him out. What did you do after that?'

'We are in the living room. Pierre says the party is over and people go away. Pierre, he is still angry and says we will settle things, but Barbara is crying, she is hysterical. So I take her to the bathroom and say I am sorry, it is all my fault.'

'When your husband said he would settle things, was Robert Banister in the room?'

'Yes, he had come in and was standing by the door. He is still strange, I do not think he knows what he is doing.'

'And what do you think your husband meant by that phrase about settling things?'

Lucille shook her head. In the end her reply was a whisper. 'I think he was going to fight again with Robert.' Still in a voice hardly raised above a whisper, she said she had still been in the bathroom trying to comfort Barbara when she had heard shouts, a cry, then a crash. She had gone in the living room to find Robert semi-conscious just beside the french window, and no sign of Pierre. Then she had gone to the balcony.

Robert's counsel was very small, superficially like Pierre in appearance, so that he felt at times disconcertingly as if he was being represented by the dead man. The little man's manner was aggressive, and in wig and gown he resembled a yapping French poodle. He was pertinacious in cross-examining Lucille, snapping away particularly at what she said and did before going into the bedroom.

'You say it was my client's glass you brought over. How do you know that?'

'I saw him put it down. I asked the waiter to refill it, then took it over to him. He drank some of it, and said he must talk to me alone.'

'You know medical examination showed my client had taken LSD.'

'I have been told, yes.'

'And it was the first time he had taken any drug. He never took drugs with you?'

'Not with me. Whether he had taken any elsewhere, I do not know.'

'I suggest you spiked the glass of wine with LSD, as a joke perhaps, to see what would happen.'

She shook her head.

'And that it was not he but you who wanted to go into the bedroom. I suggest you made love to him, not he to you, because you wanted to see what would happen when your husband came back. It was a dull party and you thought you would liven it up, wasn't that the reason?'

To these questions, and others suggesting she found it amusing to have a lover, Lucille said 'No' quietly, with lowered head. Robert found it unbearable that she should be so tormented and passed down a note: 'Stop this line of questioning.' The note was passed up to the French poodle, who ignored it, or at any rate continued with similar questions. A small quantity of some untraceable drug had been found in Pierre's body, and the poodle suggested both he and Lucille had been habitual users. This, too, she denied.

Afterward the poodle came with the solicitor to see Robert and said the cross-examination had gone well.

'Whatever happened, you knew nothing about it – you were the victim of some kind of stupid joke. And whatever happened was an accident. That's our case.'

Robert said slowly and painfully, like a man learning to speak, 'You shouldn't have said those things. When it's over, you see, Lucille and I will get married.'

The poodle stared at him, did not comment. 'I shan't be calling your wife. She was in the bathroom with Mrs Delaporte when it happened, she couldn't say anything that would help. And I'm afraid she's bitter – I don't know what the other side might make of her.'

Robert nodded, without interest.

'Now, about your own evidence—'

Robert took little interest in that, either. Carefully led by the poodle, he stumbled through his story, admitting he had fallen in love with Lucille but otherwise mentioning her as little as possible, saying he had never taken drugs, he was a peace-loving man not inclined to quarrel – when Pierre had found them in the bedroom, there had been no mention of the cufflink, and he had no recollection of what happened after being knocked unconscious.

The cross-examination that followed was no less deadly for being urbane. He talked about being 'in love', prosecuting counsel said, but wasn't it a case rather of the seduction of a lonely young woman who had become infatuated with him, the extent of that infatuation being shown by the purchase of those valuable diamond studs? He had said nothing to his wife and had hidden the studs – didn't that indicate the sordidness of the affair? At the party he had been talking to two of the dead man's close collaborators, both now under arrest. Did he expect the jury to believe drugs were not mentioned? Had he perhaps said it might be fun to try something? Increasingly, as the questions flowed on, they seemed unreal, altogether unconnected with the life and personality of that Robert Banister, an accountant at Multiplex, who had unwisely moved from Quinton Close to Marlborough Court.

The judge's summing up, although equally urbane, was unfavourable to the defendant. Nobody could doubt that Pierre Delaporte's death came about as the result of a quarrel over the affections of a beautiful though perhaps rather bored young woman, the man on high said. The only question to be decided was whether it was a pure accident or the result of an attack by the defendant, in which case he would be guilty of manslaughter. The defendant had said the cufflink had not been mentioned, but the fact that it was found beside the body was proof enough that Delaporte was aware of his wife's unfaithfulness. He mentioned the respective sizes of the men and the marks on the dead man's neck caused by an apparent attempt at strangulation, and told the jury not to draw any conclusion from the fact that the accused man's wife had not been called as a witness.

Juries, however, are not slow to make the assumption that a wife not called to give evidence in such a case can have nothing favourable to say of her husband. They took only ninety minutes to find Robert Banister guilty of manslaughter. The judge said that in view of his previously unblemished character, and some doubt about the means by which he obtained the drug he took and under whose influence he had acted, he was minded to be lenient. He passed a sentence of two years' imprisonment, of which eighteen months would be suspended. Since Robert had already been four months in prison before the trial, this meant he had only a few weeks to serve. They were the longest of his life, and during them he learned that Barbara was suing for divorce. He did not contest the case.

When he came out of prison, Robert changed his surname to Stair, moved to another part of the city, and set up as an accountant specializing in taxation matters. He wrote to Lucille at Marlborough Court, telling her he still loved her and asking if they could meet, but the letter was returned marked GONE AWAY, NO ADDRESS. A few months later, he proposed marriage to a widow who had come to him for help with her income-tax problems, and was accepted. They bought a house in Forest Gardens, a recently built estate that very much resembled Quinton Close, and settled there happily.

The two women who lived at the villa in Monaco bought with Pierre's money never talked about the past. They enjoyed, or Lucille enjoyed, the lazy life, the clothes they bought, and the trips they took together, the fact that there was never any need to worry about money or about men.

Lucille had loved Barbara from the moment that she looked up in the dentist's chair and saw that heavy, frowning face bent over her. It had begun then, when Barbara had asked abruptly whether she would like to meet again. And it was not only love she felt, but admiration for a will and intelligence much greater than her own.

For it had all been Barbara's idea and Barbara's plan, from the time Lucille learned the apartment next to theirs was vacant and said casually that it would be so much easier to spend time with each other if they were neighbours. Barbara had told her what to do, she had played her part perfectly (Barbara had said so), and now she was entirely happy. So she assured herself. Yet there were moments when she saw those heavy brows knitted and something like a scowl on the handsome face, moments when she remembered those powerful hands forcing little Pierre over the balcony while Robert lay semi-conscious on the floor. In those moments she felt afraid.

The Dream
is Better

1: Andrew Blood's Manuscript

I think of the misery of the past and the peace of the present.
I think of the women who almost blasted my life, Jean and
Olga, and then of Helen, who has brought me happiness.

In retrospect, the past seems to have been nothing but
a series of defeats and humiliations. I know the need to put
them down on paper. Helen is here today and sits on the
other side of the room. I tell her of my intention and she
approves with the serenity that is her nature. Jean and Olga
were furious, frantic, and deceitful. I had thought that to be
the nature of all women except my mother, but Helen has
shown me otherwise. She brings to my mind Edgar Allan
Poe's lines:

> *Helen, thy beauty is to me*
> *Like those Nicean barks of yore,*
> *That gently, o'er a perfumed sea,*
> *The weary, wayworn wanderer bore*
> *To his own native shore.*

With Helen I am at peace. It is not my fault that such
peace has been reached through travail and through blood.
The last may be thought appropriate, since my name is
Andrew John Blood.

My father was an inspector in the revenue service, what

is sometimes called an income-tax collector, although of course he did not collect taxes in person but was responsible only for assessing the sums owing and sending out the necessary notices. The occupation is respectable but not popular, and boys at school would jeer at me because of it. The combination of my surname and my father's occupation led them to call me bloodsucker.

'Watch out, don't let him get near you, he'll suck your blood!' they would cry. 'My dad says it's what his dad does for a living!' They would go on to make sucking noises, so that often I ran home in tears. My mother comforted me and said that they were only teasing.

It would have been useless to speak to my father. He had only two interests in life, his work and his stamp collection. He was especially concerned with nineteenth-century stamps of Chile, Peru, and Ecuador, and engaged in long correspondence about them. Once, when I was making a drawing, I knocked over the India ink I was using and ruined several pages of stamps. He showed no outward anger but afterwards had as little to do with me as possible. I have affections – yes, indeed I have affections, and of the purest kind – but I could feel no emotion when he stepped absentmindedly off the pavement one day (his mind perhaps on some Peruvian stamp issue), was knocked over by a lorry and instantly killed. After the funeral my mother said that I must be the man of the house and look after her now. I was thirteen years old.

What can I say about Mother? Her photograph, in an old-fashioned silver frame, is on the table at which I write. Her head is a little to one side, and she has the wistful and apologetic expression that I remember so well. Looking at the photograph, I see that she was a pretty woman. I was always said to look like her and be a pretty child, but this never occurred to me at the time, I suppose because for years I was so close to her.

I was an only child and she fussed over me, making sure

that I always had clean linen, cooking and washing up, keeping my bedroom tidy and making the bed. Even when I got my first job as an apprentice draughtsman in a big engineering firm (I had always been good at making neat, accurate drawings), I never had to dry a plate or a dish, and never hung up a jacket or put away a pair of shoes. My mother had said that I must look after her, but what she meant was that with my father gone she would have more time to look after me. We were constant companions and needed nobody else.

We lived in a small town in the south-east of England. Our house was about forty years old, with a bow window in front, a living room, dining room, and three bedrooms. It was a replica of the others in the road, for they had all been built at the same time. Here I lived for the first thirty years of my life.

Looking back on that time, which seems very long ago, I cannot say I was unhappy. I enjoyed my work in the drawing office of my firm. I bought a small car and used it to take Mother for a spin in the country and dinner at a little country inn, or to go with her to the town repertory theatre. She was fond of a good play.

Occasionally, late at night in my room, I wrote poems about girls, visionary girls who were an ideal for me as they were for Poe. In no way did they resemble the coarse creatures I met at the office, with their constant giggling and their vulgar jokes. Such girls were no worse than the men, but I expected that they would be better.

I was twenty-seven years of age when I met Jean.

My mother liked to go to the Conservative Party bazaar. This was held during the summer, in the grounds of Ampleton House, home of Lord and Lady Ampleton. The stalls were erected on the big central lawn, but there were tree-lined avenues on either side, down which one could walk, with little paths off them that led to cunningly created arbours and small waterfalls.

It was an enchanting place. Of course, Mother expected me to accompany her but, once arrived, she soon found people she knew and on this occasion immediately met Mrs Wilson, the Party secretary. I knew that she was occupied for at least half an hour, so that I was free to wander. I walked down one of the avenues, and then stood still at the vision I saw at the other end of it.

The avenue sloped upwards and the girl I saw was at the top of the slope, so that she was outlined against the blue sky. Her figure was slim and elegant, her bright golden hair was shoulder length, and her distant profile – for she was turned away from me – looked exquisitely delicate. I made no approach to her, for at that moment all I wanted was to keep this perfection in my memory. But she began to move towards me and to my surprise smiled and waved a hand. When we were a yard or two apart, she spoke to me by name and told me that she was Jean Merton.

She laughed, a low musical sound. 'You won't know me but I've heard a lot about you. I'm Mrs Wilson's niece.'

When seen so close she lacked the perfection of beauty I had imagined from a distance, but there was a charm and eagerness about her that overwhelmed me. Her eyes danced with pleasure and she said outright how delighted she was to meet me.

'Aunt Wilson would bring me along, though I knew it would be an awful drag. But now it's different. Come and help me buy jam and honey – I said I'd take some back. And I've got to get a bit of something or other for my young sister, Nancy. She likes bright and gaudy bits of jewellery.' She took my hand as though that was the most natural thing in the world, and it seemed natural to me also.

We bought half a dozen things at the fair, including a one-eyed elephant Jean said she must have because he looked so pathetic, and by the time we found Mrs Wilson and my mother I knew I was in love. If you think that is ridiculous you fail to understand the spell that may be cast by beauty. I had learned various facts about Jean – that she had some sort of secretarial job, was four years younger than me, and so on – but they were unimportant. She was the most beautiful person I had ever seen, and I wanted to be with her always.

I said something of this to my mother when we returned home. She listened with a smile that changed to a frown. When I had done, she said, 'Andrew, you are twenty-seven years old. How many girls have you taken out?'

'None. There was nobody I liked.'

'Your father died before telling you things you should have known. And then, perhaps I have been selfish. I had hoped we would always be together until . . .' Her voice faltered. I told her that of course I would never leave her, but she continued.

'You are an unworldly boy, a dreamer. That has always been so, and I would not wish you different. From what I hear, I am not sure that Jean Merton is the right girl for you. Perhaps there is no right girl. You may find that girls are not like your dreams, that always the dream is better.'

I had hardly listened. I had already arranged to take Jean to a concert the following evening.

In the following days I took Jean to the concert, to a travelling art exhibition that had come to our Town Hall, and to the cinema – a film with Woody Allen she wanted to see. After the film we went to dinner at the Venezia, which was said to be the best restaurant in town. I cannot remember what we ate and drank. There remains in my mind only the vision of her on the other side of the table, her laugh, her flickering fingers as she made a point about the film, her hair shining gold, whether in daylight at the art exhibition or in the subdued light of the Venezia.

Her family home was a little way outside town. She did not live there but in a small block of flats near the town centre. When I took her back that night she invited me in,

saying that she had a bottle of cognac. I said that I had
drunk both a glass of sherry and some wine.

'Don't be so *stuffy*, Andrew. Come up anyway.'

The apartment was small, a bed-sitting room, kitchen-
ette and bath. She poured the brandy, then came and sat
beside me.

'Andrew.'

'Yes?'

'You like me, don't you? If you like me, kiss me.' I put
an arm round her and our lips met, hers pressed against
mine.

'I shall begin to think you *don't* like me,' she murmured,
and the words seemed to break the bond that had kept me
almost silent. I said that liking was not the word, that for
me she was a thing of beauty, and that beautiful things
should be worshipped. She ran a hand through my hair and
said that I was a funny boy, she'd never met anybody like
me.

I drove home that night in a daze. On the following
night I asked Jean to marry me.

We had spent part of the evening in the lounge bar of
the County Hotel. Jean liked sitting in pubs and bars, saying
that they had a wonderful atmosphere. She was fond of a
drink called a whisky sour, which looked pleasant but
seemed to me to have a curious taste. I thought that she
both drank and smoked too much.

That night she seemed nervous, lighting cigarettes and
putting them out half-smoked. I asked what was the matter
and she said that her work was boring – sometimes she felt
she couldn't face it for another day.

At that I spoke. The words came out of their own
volition. 'Why not give it up?'

'What do you mean?'

'Give it up. Marry me.'

I put down the pen now and visualize the scene clearly
– a scene utterly remote from this little room. The bar was

dim, with purple-shaded wall lights. Canned music played softly. Jean's features were slightly blurred, in a way that enhanced her beauty. Her gaze looked beyond me, as though she saw our future together. She said nothing, and I was content to let the moment rest.

Then a man's voice spoke from behind my left ear. 'Who's this?' it said.

'Jerry,' Jean said. 'Jerry Wilson, this is Andrew Blood. Andrew has just asked me to marry him.' The man gave a kind of snort. 'And I've said yes,' she told him.

'Don't be bloody stupid.' The man took his hands out of his pockets. They were large and covered with hair, like a monkey's. He used obscene words to her, words I shall not write down, and was gone.

I should have known the truth then, although I could not have imagined all of it. Jean said that the man was somebody she used to know and that he was really rather awful. She also said again that she would marry me.

'You are making a mistake,' my mother said when I told her. 'I don't say that only because I shall miss you. She is not Miss Right. I could tell you things I have heard—'

I refused to listen to them.

We went together to buy the engagement ring, a simple circle of diamonds. I met her father and mother. He was a farmer and evidently well-to-do. They were polite to me, but seemed to greet the news with some reserve, which was a matter of indifference to me.

I have never cared for other people or felt the need of friends, having always been content with life at home, but I told my colleagues in the drawing office. There were congratulations, mixed with the kind of jokes I dislike, although I endured them. The department manager called me in, congratulated me, said that they were pleased with my work and that my salary would be raised. He said also that he and the rest of them hoped to meet my future wife. I made some reply, I don't know what. I had no wish that

Jean should meet any of them. My private life had nothing to do with my work.

The engagement was announced in the local paper. I saw Jean most evenings and she often came to lunch on Sunday. Mother was an excellent cook, took special pains with these lunches, and was polite to Jean, but I could see it was all on the surface.

Jean said more than once that Mother didn't like her.

'She doesn't want to lose her pretty baby boy. And she thinks I smoke too much – I can see her counting the number of cigarettes each time I light one.' Of course I said that wasn't true, although I knew there was something in it. 'And she expects to be paid compliments every time she cooks a meal. I can cook, you know. I'll make dinner for us tomorrow night.'

And she did. Each of the courses was from a recipe originated by a great chef and had some complicated sauce or dressing. I really preferred mother's simpler cooking, but of course I said everything was wonderful. Afterwards we sat on the sofa. I kissed her, and within a few moments she made a suggestion to me which, again, I shall not write down, accompanying it with physical actions. I said as gently as possible that I did not care for or approve that kind of thing, certainly not until we were married.

She lay back and stared at me. I could see that she was angry, but anger made her more beautiful than ever. She said I had better go home, and I left her.

I heard nothing from her after that. I telephoned her office and was told that she was on a week's holiday. I rang the flat but there was no reply.

When the week had passed, she called and said that she would like to see me. The place was the lounge of the County Hotel, where I had proposed to her. When I arrived she was already there, a whisky sour in front of her. She pushed a little box across to me.

'One ring, returned,' she said. 'Engagement finished.'

I stared at her unbelievingly.

'It was a mistake. I should never have said yes. You want to know why I did? You'll hardly believe it in these days of the pill – or perhaps you've never heard of the pill, I'd forgotten what you're like – but Jerry had got me pregnant. He didn't want the kid and I did, or I thought so. So when you turned up I said yes. I was going to try to make you believe the kid was yours, but there wasn't much chance of that, was there? I don't think I could have gone through with it anyway, but it doesn't matter now. I had an abortion. Jerry and I are getting married.'

I took the ring and looked at it wonderingly. I could feel tears forming in my eyes, tears not of self-pity but of regret at losing so much beauty. Jean finished her drink.

'It would never have done, and you must know that. I like the way you look, but you don't really need anyone but your mother.'

That was the end of it. I told Mother that the engagement was broken. She said that she was pleased for my sake and with her wonderful discretion never uttered another word about it. I sold the ring back for half what I paid for it. There were jokes at the office, but I ignored them and after a while they stopped. I have said already that I had no close friends.

Mother and I settled down to our old life together. She said sometimes that Miss Right would come along one day, although she hoped it would be after she had gone. Sometimes she added that this might not be long. I told her not to talk like that and paid no attention to what she said.

Then one day, nearly two years after the parting from Jean, I came home and found Mother dead. It seemed that she had a heart condition of which she had never told me. She had gone upstairs to lie down in the afternoon, as she often did, and had passed out of life without pain.

I was stunned. In the days and weeks that followed I

realized how much I had depended upon her for everything. I knew I must change my life. I sold the house, got rid of the furniture and most of Mother's possessions, although I could not bring myself to dispose of some things, like her jewellery. That was a terrible time and I cannot write more about it.

The doctor was concerned for me and said that I should go away to recover from the shock. I did so, and found Helen. Again, I shall not write about this. When I returned I bought an apartment and lived there contentedly. Through Helen I have learned to cook, to wash and iron clothes, and through her the flat is kept in a way that would have made Mother proud. I never spoke of her to the people I worked with, feeling it was better so.

So passed weeks, and months. I have made what happened sound sudden but it was gradual. I recovered from the shocks of Jean's betrayal and Mother's death, like somebody slowly emerging from severe illness who becomes a little stronger each day. With Helen's help I recovered my serenity so that the past was wiped out as though it had never been.

And then Olga entered my life – Olga from central Europe, Olga Kreisky.

Olga's parents had been refugees who came to this country just before the war, and although she was born in England she spoke with a distinct foreign accent. She had some architectural training and came to the office as a draughtsman. She was a large woman, large in a way that people call motherly, although my mother had been fine-boned and delicate, as I am.

Olga was, I suppose, about my own age, although because of her size she seemed to me older. I do not know why she should have taken an interest in me, but she did so from the beginning. She would sit at the same table with me in the canteen and would say that I did not eat enough, I should have ordered the batter pudding or the macaroni and cheese. I would reply that I was not hungry and in any case did not care for starchy foods.

'But you are so thin, And-rew' – almost from the start she called me Andrew, dwelling lovingly on the name. 'You should put flesh on your bones. It is because you cook for yourself, that is not good. A man on his own never eats properly.'

She told me she lived with her sister, who would be getting married soon. 'Then I am on my own too, but never fear, I shall go on making my soups and puddings, and my schnitzels. You must come round, And-rew, and I cook for you my special wiener schnitzel. You will not feel hungry afterwards, I can tell you.' She laughed heartily and her plump cheeks wobbled.

Mother taught me always to be polite and I hope I have not forgotten my manners. I said I had a poor digestion and must be very careful. She said she knew of many special health foods and she could prepare those too. I stopped using the canteen, but it did not free me from her. She would come over to my drawing board to see what I was working on and, leaning over so that I felt the pressure of her bosom, praise my skill and neatness.

She made sure that she left the office when I did, and at first I made the foolish mistake of giving her a lift in my car, with the result that I was invited indoors to meet her sister. She introduced me as 'My dear friend And-rew' and her sister Nadia said she had heard much about me. How could she have done when there was nothing to hear? I stopped driving to work in the car.

Olga wanted to see my flat, saying she was sure it needed a woman's touch. I avoided giving her the address. I knew it would be disastrous for her to meet Helen. I had to endure a great deal of what I believe is called 'ribbing' about Olga at the office. I said nothing, I showed my supreme indifference, both to the dolts surrounding me and to Olga, but Olga's skin was hippopotamus-thick. She began to bring pies and sandwiches to the office, insisting that we share them for lunch. I did not know how to refuse without rudeness. I nearly told her of Helen at home, who would prepare anything I wished, but refrained.

The strain on my nerves grew. I thought of changing my job, but feared that Olga might follow me elsewhere. Her round fat face, her huge udders, the whole bulk of her began to obsess me. I had nightmares in which the weight of her flesh bore me down, so that I wriggled unavailingly beneath her. Yet I could not have imagined the nightmare that happened.

I had returned from work at the usual time, looking forward to my evening at home with Helen. A steak and salad, cheese and coffee, then an hour or two in front of the television. When the bell rang, Helen answered it. That was a mistake, for outside stood Olga, her arms full of brown paper parcels. It was dark in the hall, so that at first she did not see she was speaking to Helen.

'And-rew, I have been a naughty girl. You will not tell me your address, it is not in the phone-book, but I get it from the accounts department. But you forgive me, And-rew, when you see what I have here for us to eat. There is smoked salmon and then a special Hungarian sausage with noodles—'

At that moment she realized she was talking to Helen. And she began to laugh.

Her laughter roused me to fury. If she had not laughed I might have told her just to go away. But she laughed, this fat European cow laughed at my Helen. I pulled her inside the door and then towards the kitchen. She dropped the groceries. Then we were in the kitchen. I took the knife with which I had been trimming the steak and plunged it into the fat creature who had insulted Helen.

I cannot say what else I did with the knife. I was sane before the action, I am perfectly sane now, but I admit that for those moments I was mad. Mad, but greatly provoked. I do not excuse my action, yet surely all must agree that I was greatly provoked. When it was over, and the screaming had stopped, I looked at the thing on the floor and saw blood, blood everywhere. I felt that this was something ordained, that I had fulfilled my name. There had been eggs among the groceries and they had broken, so that in one place the yellow egg yolks were mixed with the red blood. When the police came I was trying to clear up the mess on the kitchen floor.

Such are the events that brought me to this room. I have set them down at Dr Glasser's suggestion, and should like to add that I am happy to have retired from the world and grateful for the opportunity to live here and to receive visits from Helen.

2: *The Ironies of Dr Glasser*

Dr Glasser's office was large and square. The walls were white and covered with framed certificates testifying to the doctor's psychiatric eminence. In person the doctor was tall, with an aquiline nose and a fine head of grey hair. There was something ironical in his gaze and in his manner, as though he found the world even more absurd than he had expected.

His visitor – small, tubby, with innocent eyes behind gold-rimmed spectacles – was named Johnson. He was a vice-president of the Mental Patients' Reform League. He put down the sheets of paper, which were written in a neat and elegant hand.

'Most interesting. And remarkably coherent, it seems to me.'

'Yes, Andrew is perfectly coherent. It is a classic case, textbook material.' Dr Glasser steepled his fingers and looked up at the ceiling, as though he were lecturing. 'The child is ignored by the father, attachment to the mother becomes total. Every woman met is seen not as a real person but in terms of the mother. Because of the incest taboo the sex act cannot be contemplated with any woman, they must all be remade in the mother's image. The experience with Jean was unfortunate, but it would have been much the same with any woman who desired sexual relations. For the reasons I have given, the sex act fills Andrew with horror.'

Mr Johnson moved uneasily. 'I understand. But my point is—'

Dr Glasser in flow was not easily checked. 'He rejects it with violence. The injuries inflicted on poor Olga Kreisky were savage, far more than is indicated in the manuscript. There were mutilations.'

'Very distressing. But all this was several years ago.'

'Six years.'

'As you know, the League's concern is that far too many patients are kept in homes, when they would be perfectly capable of leading normal lives. I understand Andrew still makes technical drawings.'

'He does indeed. Very good ones.'

'So that he is obviously capable of work. From his record, his behaviour here has been exemplary. If he were let out on condition that he lives with this Helen, who I suppose might be called a mother-substitute, and to whom he is evidently devoted, would he be a danger to the community? But first, would you agree that Helen is a mother-substitute?'

The doctor turned his ironical gaze on Mr Johnson. 'I would.'

'And would he be a danger to other people?'

'Perhaps not.'

Mr Johnson took off his glasses, polished them, and said earnestly, 'Only perhaps? You agreed that his behaviour has been exemplary?'

'I did.'

'Then why should he not be released?'

146

'Suppose somebody else insulted Helen?'

Mr Johnson was taken aback. 'Why should that happen? Helen has been remarkably faithful to him – she is clearly devoted. I understand from the document that she pays visits. Perhaps they might marry.'

Dr Glasser sighed. 'Come along, Mr Johnson. We will speak to this exemplary patient.'

They left the room, took a lift, walked down a corridor, then down another at right angles to it. On either side were doors with names on them. The doors had keyholes but lacked handles. In a room between the corridors four male nurses sat playing cards. Little Mr Johnson was uneasily conscious that they were all big men. The doctor spoke to one of them, who accompanied them. He opened one of the doors with a key from a bunch at his waist and said, 'Andrew, here's Dr Glasser to see you.'

They entered a small sitting room, simply furnished. Several drawings were pinned up on the walls, some of machinery, one of Dr Glasser, and two of a woman Mr Johnson supposed to be Helen. A man who sat reading in an armchair put down his book. He was small and had neat, almost doll-like features. 'Good afternoon, Doctor.'

'Andrew, this is Mr Johnson from the Mental Patients' Reform League. He enjoyed your manuscript.'

'Did you really? I'm so pleased.' A smile touched the neat features. 'It's all true, you know, every word. I was provoked, but I did very wrong. Just for the moment I went mad, although I am perfectly sane now, have been for years. Look at what I'm reading.' He held up the book. '*Persuasion*, Jane Austen. I like to read about the past, it's so much more civilized than the present.'

Mr Johnson asked in his earnest way, 'Supposing you were released, would you like that?' Andrew Blood considered, then nodded. 'You would take a job, use your technical skills?' Another nod. 'And live with Helen? Perhaps get married?'

147

A look of uncertainty, even alarm, touched the neat features. Andrew Blood looked questioningly at the doctor, who said softly, 'If Helen is here, Andrew, we'd be delighted to meet her.'

The uncertain look was replaced by a charming smile. Andrew jumped up and went to an inner room. The nurse began to say something, but was checked by Dr Glasser. It was perhaps no more than two or three minutes, although it seemed longer to Mr Johnson, before the figure appeared in the doorway.

It was small and wore a wig of grey hair, permanently waved. The face below it was that of Andrew Blood, but it had been powdered to a dead whiteness and lipstick crudely applied so that it looked like a clown's face. The figure wore an oatmeal-coloured twin set with a rope of imitation pearls round the neck and high-heeled shoes. It came mincingly across the room, held out a ringed hand, and said in a falsetto voice, 'How do you do?'

The figure was ludicrous in itself, but it was the words and the falsetto voice that broke Mr Johnson's composure. He was unable to refrain from laughter. The sounds were loud in the little room, and although he put a hand over his mouth laughter continued to bubble up.

That was one moment. In the next he was on the floor, hands were tearing at his face and throat, a high voice was screaming abuse. His face had been badly scratched and his spectacles knocked off, although not broken, before the doctor and nurse managed to pull the figure off him.

Back in the office Dr Glasser poured a tot of whisky and apologized. 'Forgive me for practising that little deceit. I should have told you that Andrew was Helen, but I thought visual evidence would be more convincing. Of course, I could not know that you would laugh. That was an insult to Helen, and Andrew was outraged by it, as he was when Olga Kreisky laughed.'

'And Helen is—'

'Hardly Poe's Helen, as you will have gathered from her appearance. Helen was the name of Andrew's mother. She was the centre of his life, and when she died he re-created her. Those were some of her old clothes. Andrew said in the manuscript that he could not bring himself to dispose of them. He is a small, neat man, and they fit him reasonably well.

'I told you it was a classic case and so it is, not of transvestism but of personality transfer. It occurs only among those who cannot face the physical aspects of life. Mrs Blood understood that when she told him there might be no right girl for him, that he would always be one of those for whom the dream is better.'

The Borgia
Heirloom

'And now,' Lady X said, 'you may ask your questions.'

The young man repeated, perhaps for the sixth time, that it was very good of her to receive him, and give him lunch, and talk to him. At that, she merely inclined her head, told the maid that they would take coffee in the drawing room, and led the way there. She was very old, her skin the colour of parchment, her hands liver-spotted, thickly veined, the nails yellow and horny. Several rings – a large diamond, a sapphire-and-ruby cluster, a huge emerald – looked incongruous on them.

'It's not exactly questions.' The young man was American, his fair hair cut close to the head, his eyes round and innocent, his manner earnest. 'I'm doing this book on great unsolved British cases, they're so much subtler than our crude shootouts, and I'm trying to get accounts from people who actually knew the background and the characters. Official accounts don't really bring them to life.'

'I can do that for you.' Her laugh was a raven's caw, but she shook her head when, with a tentative air, he produced a notebook. 'Oh, no – no. Notebooks are for reporters, my dear young man. I understand you to be a real writer.'

He put away the notebook. He had, after all, a good memory.

'The place, as you know, was Gratchen Manor, where

we are now – the home of my husband's family for more than a century. It is a pleasant place, one with an ambience that impresses itself on the characters of those who live in it. Do you understand me?'

The young American nodded. In truth, he was overawed by the great house, the portraits of grim-faced ancestors along the walls, the intimidating size of the dining room in which the two of them had eaten at one end of the long table, and of this drawing room with its grand piano, alcoves containing what was no doubt immensely valuable porcelain, great windows looking on to a terrace from which steps led down to what seemed acres of lawn. It seemed to him wrong that families should live in such large houses – and now not even a family, but one old woman and her housekeeper, plus a servant or two.

'This house and this English countryside formed the character of my husband, Tom, and our son Charlie. You would have had to know them to understand them. Tom – Sir Thomas – went to London two or three days each week, he was a director of this company and vice-chairman of that, but his heart was here at Gratchen. He took part in every local event, thought of himself as the squire, as his father and grandfather had been before him, employed half the people in the village, felt responsible for their moral welfare. A strange thing that, in this modern world, but it was so.'

The young man nodded. He had heard different tales in the village, where Sir Thomas was resented as a man who poked his nose into matters that did not concern him.

'And Charlie, Charlie was perfect. Everybody loved him.' She indicated a portrait, head and shoulders, of a weakly handsome young man in officer's uniform. 'I prayed for him to come through the War unharmed, and my prayers were answered. Then all I wanted was for him to marry the right girl and make this house their home. That will sound old-fashioned, too, I'm sure.'

Charlie's fellow officers had said he was pleasant

enough, but thick as two blocks. Feeling that he should speak, the young American said, 'That was in nineteen forty-eight.'

'I believe so.' Lady X's small eyes were sharp within their folds of skin. 'I hope you do not expect dates and hours. This is a mystery without a solution. I am telling you what happened, no more.

'In the autumn, Charlie became engaged to Susan Baybridge. They had known each other from childhood, her father was a barrister, it was a suitable match in every way.' Lady X rose arthritically, took a silver-framed photograph from the top of the grand piano, and showed it to the young man. 'That was Susan at the time.'

The photograph showed a rather plain, heavy-featured girl with a determined chin. 'Charlie was involved in some kind of commercial activity in London, which his father seemed to think necessary. He came back here, of course, at weekends. You may imagine my incredulity when he arrived one weekend in company with a young woman and told us he intended to break his engagement with Susan and marry this – this woman. Her name was Deirdre O'Connor and she was alleged to be a fashion model. It was obvious to me at once that she was out for what she could get and had no feeling for Charlie. It was found later that she had granted her favours to half a dozen young men.

'I thought her an entirely unsuitable wife for Charlie, and told him so, and I told him also that his treatment of Susan was disgraceful. I was not surprised that when at last he told her that he wished to break off their engagement, there was a violent quarrel. In front of the servants.'

In front of the servants, he thought. It was certainly a different world. As if reading his thoughts, she said, 'It was another world we lived in here at Gratchen. And a better one.

'In the New Year, we gave a dinner party. Of course we invited Susan. She did some job in a scientific laboratory and we invited the director of the place, a tiresome man named Cleggit. There were other friends, including our local medical man, Dr MacFarlane – a dozen altogether. Then, quite unexpectedly, Charlie came down, the woman with him. Susan had to meet the woman – it was most unpleasant for her.'

'Your son said he told you he was coming down and you must have forgotten.'

'I forget nothing.' Her gaze was withering. 'May I continue? Thank you. We ate simple English food, which, even in those days of rationing, was not denied to us at Gratchen. A clear soup made with stock, roast beef accompanied by the usual vegetables, an apple charlotte. It was not a happy meal. Tom was already sick with the kidney disease from which he died six months later, Susan hardly spoke, the dreadful Deirdre talked too much and too loudly, and Charlie was obviously besotted by her. After dinner we came in here, and it was then that Deirdre behaved as if drunk or drugged. She staggered about, almost fell over when sitting down in a chair, a disgusting exhibition. Then she collapsed and was taken to lie down, Dr MacFarlane attending her. He agreed with me that she had taken an overdose of drugs, and when we questioned Charlie he admitted that she used both cocaine and heroin. She was taken ill at nine-thirty. Just after midnight, she died.'

'But drugs didn't cause her death.'

'Dr MacFarlane thought so at the time.'

'But Cleggit knew better. His pharmaceutical knowledge led him to suspect an alkaloid poison. He made sure that the wine glasses and coffee cups were preserved, not washed up.'

'Cleggit was a busybody, a troublemaker.'

'And you know what was found in one coffee cup. Coniine, the drug derived from *conium maculatum*, the spotted hemlock. The poison Socrates took, the drug Keats said induced a drowsy numbness, the drug of which even a few drops may be a fatal dose. But how was it administered? That was what the police could never establish. It must have been from some kind of phial, but none was found. Your son poured the coffee, you added sugar, but none of the guests noticed anything unusual, and in any case Deirdre O'Connor took no sugar.'

The maid came in with a tray containing a coffee pot, two cups, a milk jug, and a bowl of sugar cubes. The young man continued. 'Of course, there were suspects. Susan had reason enough to hate Deirdre. Your son might have found out about her other men friends. It was even suggested that your husband, knowing himself under sentence of death, might have been responsible.'

'That was ridiculous. If Cleggit had not been such a busybody, Dr MacFarlane would have signed a death certificate. As it was, the affair broke up the family. Charlie went out to Australia, married a girl there, died five years ago without an heir. I am quite alone now.'

The young man's eyes were bright. He lowered his voice, almost whispered, as he said, 'You arranged the dinner party, you knew your son was coming, you invited Dr MacFarlane. I think you did it.'

She seemed not to have heard him, poured the coffee into the two cups. 'It was all so long ago. Do you take milk?'

'What? Oh no, thank you.'

'Sugar?'

'No sugar.' He leaned forward. 'Won't you tell me, now that it can do no harm, just for my satisfaction as an amateur criminologist, how you did it?'

The little eyes in the wrinkled face were amused, contemptuous. 'You are an impertinent young man. I said I was telling you a story to which there is no solution.' She passed him the coffee cup, then held up her veined, spotted hand with the bright rings on it. 'Would you believe that my hands were once admired? Nowadays people only look

155

at the rings. The emerald is an heirloom, said to have belonged to a Borgia.'

What followed was so quick that if she had not drawn attention to her hand he would not have seen it. From the centre of the great emerald ring a tiny stream of liquid shot into her cup. She gave her raven caw at his shocked, startled face and said, 'Liquid saccharin.'

Did Sherlock Holmes Meet Hercule—?

Did Sherlock Holmes ever meet Hercule Poirot? It is their possible encounter that gives peculiar interest to the following story, found among the papers of Poirot's friend Captain Arthur Hastings, who recorded a number of the great Belgian detective's cases. Why should an affair involving Sherlock Holmes and narrated by Dr Watson be among the Hastings papers? Perhaps the narrative itself answers the question. It is unfortunately not quite complete, but there can be no more than a single page missing at the end.

Sherlock Holmes would shake his head when I mentioned the name of Mulready and say the world was not yet prepared to hear about an affair that involved a chief Minister of the Crown, secret papers, and the threat of war. Yet it can do no harm to set down the extraordinary series of events involving the inhabitants of Mulready House while they remain fresh in my mind.

It was an autumn morning a couple of years before Holmes's retirement, and I had spent the night with my old friend in Baker Street. Breakfast was finished, he had done with the papers, and was roaming about the room, talking discursively as was his wont, when he stopped at the window.

'Halloa, Watson. Our humble lodgings are about to be unusually honoured.'

'Holmes, if you are going to give me some of those far-fetched deductions about—'

Holmes laughed. 'No, no, my dear fellow. It is true that when I see a man being driven up in the latest model of Rolls-Royce motorcar, and when that vehicle has a crest on the door panel, I know a person of some distinction is likely to step out of it. But in fact I recognized the man himself. It is Lord Rivington.'

A moment later, our Secretary for War was in the room. His features were familiar to me through many photographs and cartoons, but none had done full justice to the force in those craggy features, the intensity of the deep-set eyes behind the bushy brows. He looked from one of us to the other.

'Mr Holmes, I have come to ask your help in a matter of great importance, and one that is absolutely confidential.'

I rose, but Holmes stopped me. 'You may speak in Dr Watson's presence as freely as you would if I were alone.'

'Nevertheless . . .' Sherlock Holmes was filling his pipe. He said nothing. Lord Rivington looked at him fiercely, then shrugged. 'Very well, there is no time for argument. You are aware that negotiations are going on between this country and France that involve a plan for joint action if the Kaiser's sabre-rattling should turn to the drawing of swords?'

'I know what is said in the newspapers, nothing more.'

'The negotiations have reached a most delicate stage. You can imagine my feelings when I discovered through our Intelligence Service that everything we have discussed was known in Berlin, down to the last detail. And it was shown to me quite inescapably that the information must have reached Germany through the office of the man in charge of the negotiations, Sir Charles Mulready. He is one of my oldest friends, we were at school and the Varsity together. I could swear that he is a man of honour. Yet these papers have passed through no hands but his. You may ask how I can be so sure of this, Mr Holmes. The answer is simple. I heard it yesterday from Sir Charles's own lips.'

'Nobody in his office had access to them?'

'Nobody. They were kept in a safe, and were under lock and key when he took them home. And there has been no betrayal from the French side.' Lord Rivington coughed. 'Allies may have their own secrets. Certain matters mentioned in memoranda accompanying the documents have not been discussed with the French, yet these, too, are known in Berlin. They have not been stolen, hence they must have been either copied or photographed.'

Holmes had been following with the keenest attention. 'Does Sir Charles have any family links with Germany?'

'There you've hit it, Mr Holmes. He married a German lady who had been left a widow with a young son when her husband, Count von Brankel, was killed in a hunting accident. The boy, Hans, has been brought up as if he were Charles's own son. He is intelligent, but I fear not manly. He was expelled from his public school – I am sure I need not enter into details. Then he studied medicine for a year, but gave it up and expressed a wish to become a stage actor, something which of course could not be countenanced. Accordingly, he follows no profession, lives at home, and sponges on his family. They have a daughter of their own, Lilian, who has some ridiculous idea that women should be allowed to vote, and that what she calls weapons of murder should be abolished. My friends have not been fortunate in their children.'

'One more question. Am I right in thinking that our French allies would be interested in the memoranda they have not seen?'

For a moment the Secretary for War looked surprised. 'Possibly, but the relations between our countries are entirely friendly. Monsieur Calamy, who is handling the negotiations, is in London and staying at Mulready House.'

Holmes nodded.

'And now I come to the tragic climax. A draft known as Plan X has been prepared, setting out in detail our military and naval commitments to France in the event of war. Together with it was a memorandum about the defence of Britain which was for our eyes only, not those of M. Calamy. Both of these were in Sir Charles's possession. Yesterday, when what had been suspicions became certainties, I asked him to come and see me. He had been away from Whitehall corridors for a couple of days with an attack of gout, but he limped along to see me, and I told him what I had learned.

'He behaved as I would have expected, was first incredulous and then horrified. He protested his innocence, and I believed him.' The great head bent down for a moment, then he looked from one of us to the other in despair. 'Yet last night he made a confession of guilt, not in words but in his actions. He took an overdose of a medicine he used to ease his sufferings from gout. And there is worse to say. Both Plan X and the memorandum were with him, taken home for study. Both are missing.'

A few minutes later, we were sitting in the Rolls-Royce, on the way to the Mulready home in Mayfair.

The blinds were drawn over the long windows, and within the house we felt the sombre atmosphere of sudden death. Lord Rivington led the way up to Sir Charles's suite, separated from his wife's by a dressing room.

'Lady Mulready found him in pain at some time in the night and immediately called his doctor, whose name is Cardew. He said Sir Charles must have suffered an acute attack of gout and taken an overdose of his medicine, but I fear it was taken deliberately.'

'I know Dr Cardew,' I said. 'A most reliable practitioner.' I approached the bed where the body lay, decently covered by a sheet, and looked at the distorted features. An empty glass stood on a bedside table, with a bottle beside it, perhaps one-third full, labelled *Colnatium*. 'This is a medicine often used for gout. It contains colchicum, which relieves the pain. I see no unusual circumstances here.'

'Do you not, Watson?' Holmes had been prowling the room and the dressing room beyond, examining pictures, ornaments, a pipe rack, using his magnifying glass to look closely at a bureau in the dressing room. Now he, too, lifted the sheet, then looked carefully at the glass and bottle, tipping the latter and holding it to the light.

'Colchicum is a poison, like many plants and flowers that play a part in relieving pain. Yellow jasmine, spotted hemlock, the foxglove, the Calabar bean, and the paternoster pea – these can be as deadly as the poppy or laburnum seeds. I have in preparation a little pamphlet called "The Poison Garden", which should be useful to every medical practitioner. And colchicum may ease pain in small quantities, but in larger ones it can kill. Did you remark the amount of precipitation in that bottle, Watson? It should not be there, and there are marks of sediment in the glass. Somebody added more colchicum to the bottle, and made this gout remedy a poisonous drink.'

I looked again at the bottle. 'Holmes, you are right. But how—'

'That is what we must discover. And colchicum is bitter, the first taste should have warned Sir Charles.' He turned to Lord Rivington. 'I take it that Plan X and the memorandum were kept in the dressing-room bureau. The lock has been picked skilfully, but scratches show under the magnifying glass. Perhaps we may now talk to Lady Mulready.'

The widow was a tall, stately grey-haired lady. Lord Rivington called her Ilse, and she spoke to him as Gerald. She greeted Holmes warmly.

'Mr Holmes, I know what Lord Rivington believes, but

161

I can assure you he is wrong. I am a German and proud of my ancestry, and I know my husband's equal pride in being British. Some terrible mistake has been made.'

'I believe we shall find an explanation that will be entirely honourable to his name. If you could tell me what happened yesterday after his return from Whitehall, I should be grateful.'

'My husband told me little or nothing of political affairs. When he returned home, I could see that he was upset, but he said nothing of the cause and I had learned that it was useless to ask. He remained in his private rooms until dinner. We were five at table, our children, Hans and Lilian, and M. Calamy making up the rest of the party. It was not a cheerful meal. My husband's gout was troubling him and he hardly spoke, except when Lilian provoked him by speaking of some suffragette meeting she had attended. Hans seemed preoccupied and M. Calamy was concerned, as always, with his food.'

A fleeting smile crossed her face. 'We live simply here. My husband did not care what he ate, and the years have reconciled me to English cooking, but M. Calamy cannot endure it. He has brought his chef as well as his valet, but although his meals are specially prepared he still grumbles. So he did last night. After dinner, my husband called me aside and said, "I have painful decisions to make, Ilse, and I fear the result will cause you grief." Those were his last words to me.'

'When was the tragedy discovered?'

'At three o'clock this morning. I heard cries coming from my husband's room. I went in and found him in terrible pain. Dr Cardew was summoned immediately, but by the time he arrived Charles was in a coma and he could do nothing. The end came just after seven.'

'Were your son and daughter present?'

'Lilian, yes. Hans . . .' She hesitated. 'It proved almost

impossible to rouse him and, when at last the housemaid did so, he staggered, as though under the influence of drink. Coming from his room to his father's, he slipped, fell down several stairs, and, as it proved, broke his ankle. He had to be carried back to bed, and Dr Cardew says he must stay in his room.'

'A last question, and I have done. You said your husband didn't care what he ate. Was there a special reason for that?'

'Yes. A nasal operation a few years ago almost deprived him of taste and smell, so that he could barely distinguish chicken from beef or claret from brandy. Surely that cannot be important?'

'It is one piece in the jigsaw, no more.'

Outside the drawing room, we were met by a young girl. It was easy to see this was Ilse Mulready's daughter, although there was a light in her eye and a spring in her step that her mother lacked. She held out an envelope. 'Which of you gentlemen is Mr Sherlock Holmes? Here is a letter for you.'

Holmes looked at the envelope, tore it open, read it, and passed it to me. Some words were printed in capitals on a single sheet of paper:

MISTER HOLMES GO AWAY
YOUR PRESENTS HERE IS UNNECESSARY

'Written with a Waverley nib on a standard Ranelagh-weave paper,' Holmes said. 'Was this delivered by hand, Miss Mulready?'

'No, one of the footmen found it on the hall table. What does it say?' Holmes showed it to her, and she flushed. 'I think he's right. Of course, I am sorry my father is dead, but he should be allowed to rest in peace. I know he died because he was a man of war, as you are, Lord Rivington.

He hated poor Hans, because Hans had no interest in fighting and killing people. I heard them arguing last night in Father's room.'

'And what was the subject?'

'I don't know. And if I did, I shouldn't tell you.' She turned away from us and ran upstairs. Lord Rivington coughed, hummed under his breath, said nothing.

'Surely this note is important, Holmes,' I said. 'It was obviously written by somebody almost illiterate.'

'Or somebody who wants us to think so. Or—'

He was interrupted by the appearance of a gentleman dressed with rather too obvious elegance, his hair glossy, his beard wonderfully neat. My feeling that there is something unmanly about the French is reinforced by their use of pomades and perfumes. This, of course, was M. Calamy, who now expressed his regrets to Lord Rivington, smiling as he did so.

'Perhaps after this tragedy our negotiations should be given up – postponed, as you say.'

'Not at all.' Lord Rivington spoke sharply. 'They are more than ever urgent, and I shall take charge of them in person.'

'That will make me happy. We shall, of course, conduct them on both sides with entire frankness.' The Frenchman's smile perhaps broadened a little. 'Later today I move from this house of sorrow to our Embassy.'

'With your staff?' Lord Rivington said with heavy irony.

'My valet, my chef, what should I do without them?' He bowed slightly and was gone. The Secretary for War muttered something among which I thought I heard the words 'primping popinjay'.

Holmes looked after him with a puzzled air, then stood deep in thought. Lord Rivington said impatiently, 'Mr Holmes, this is no time for brooding.'

'I beg your pardon. I agree, Plan X must be returned to you at once.'

'You know where it is?' the Secretary for War said in astonishment.

'It was an elementary problem.'

Holmes asked a maid to take us to Mr Hans's room. As we walked up the great stairs and down a long passage, Holmes murmured to me, 'Nevertheless, Watson, there is something I do not understand.'

We found the son of the house on a sofa, one foot heavily bandaged. He was a good-looking young fellow with delicate, almost pretty features, but at this moment they were taut with anguish. A bowl of flowers stood on a window ledge beside him and Holmes picked it up.

'The autumn crocus,' he said musingly. 'A charming but dangerous flower.'

The young man started, then said, 'Before God, Mr Holmes, I never intended—'

'I am prepared to believe you, but I am not your judge. Let me tell you what I think happened and you can say how nearly it approaches the truth.'

He turned to us. 'Hans here is one of those unfortunate people with a strong feminine streak that leads them into dubious, even criminal associations. Such deviations have touched our own Royal family – you will recall the need to hush up the scandal of the noble visitors to the male brothel in Cleveland Street. The German Intelligence department became aware of Han's propensities and they have been blackmailing him. He has abstracted documents from his stepfather's bureau, copied, and then returned them. When you, Lord Rivington, told Sir Charles what had happened, he knew who the culprit must be.'

The young man wrung his hands. 'They threatened to expose me. I would have gone to prison. What else could I do?'

'You should have told your step-father,' Holmes said

sternly. 'I come to the events of last night. Sir Charles called you to his room. I don't know what he said, perhaps that you must leave the country, but it made you desperate. You had sufficient medical knowledge to know that colchicum was in your stepfather's medicine, and that it is easily distilled from the autumn crocus. Perhaps you prepared it then, perhaps you had some already prepared for just such an emergency. You added it to the medicine.'

'It was to make sure he slept soundly. I swear I never meant him to die.'

'I don't suppose you did. A little medical knowledge may be not merely dangerous but fatal. Otherwise, your scheme worked well enough. You took the papers, I suppose meaning to copy and return them. Why did you not do so?'

'Because I was drugged. All you say is true, Mr Holmes, but can you explain what happened to me? When I knew my stepfather would be asleep, I went to his dressing room and took the plan and the memorandum – the bureau drawer was easy to open, I had done it before. I brought them in here to copy and return them, and then I was going to post the copy at once. But I was too sleepy, my fingers wouldn't move over the paper. I put the papers away and fell asleep, and when I was woken I felt so dizzy I could hardly stand. It was because of the dizziness that I fell and broke my ankle.' He gestured at the bandages. 'Then Dr Cardew gave me an opiate and I slept until ten o'clock this morning. Now I am told not to move.'

'The papers are still here?' Lord Rivington cried. 'Then if you want a chance of saving your villainous skin, tell me where they are.'

'In that bookcase,' the young man said sullenly. 'Behind the top row of books, on the right.'

Lord Rivington went to the bookcase, took out some books in the top row, put his hand in, took out more books, and turned with a furious face. 'There is nothing here! What trick are you trying to play?'

'Nothing?' I have never seen a ghastlier look of fear and apprehension on a man's face. 'Impossible.' He shrank back as Lord Rivington approached him threateningly.

'Wait,' Sherlock Holmes said in an imperative tone. 'Something is wrong here, there is something I have not understood.' He paced up and down the room while the rest of us watched. 'Did you write a card saying my presence here was unnecessary? I thought not, yet it came from within the house. Last night you all ate the same food at dinner?'

'Except M. Calamy. His food is specially prepared by his chef.'

'And afterwards?'

'My stepfather left us. Coffee was served, but my digestion is poor. I always have a cup of chocolate.'

'A cup of chocolate, yes. And M. Calamy was very pleased with himself. I have been stupid, Watson.'

'Holmes, I don't know what you're talking about.' I could see from Lord Rivington's expression that he was similarly bewildered.

'The card, Watson, the card. It was a Frenchman's English misspelling. But quick, there is not a moment to lose, he is leaving.'

'M. Calamy?'

'The man who drugged the cup of chocolate – his so-called chef.'

We found him in a servants' bedroom under the eaves, packing his bag for departure. He did not seem surprised to see us.

'Ah, Monsieur Holmes. Here is what you look for.' A large envelope lay on the bed. 'The excellent Plan X, and the other paper.'

'Which you have copied.'

'Precisely, *mon cher*. Now Britain and France have no

secrets from each other, we can be entirely frank in discussion.'

'It was you who sent me the postcard.'

'My spelling, she is not of the best, but that is so.'

'You drugged the chocolate, and then took the documents.'

'On behalf of la belle France. I am called the good M. Calamy's chef, but he gets the indigestion from my cooking.' He chuckled. 'I make my investigation, and soon understand that the young Hans is – like your Oscar Wilde, shall we say? – and is responsible for what has happened. And I see things are, as you say, coming to the head, so I arrange for the young Hans to have a little harmless sleep while I take possession of Plan X and the memorandum. No harm is done – except to our friend Sir Charles. That is a great tragedy.'

He was an odd-looking little fellow, very short, his head a perfect egg shape. His hair was very black and parted in the middle, his moustaches long and pointed. He wore patent-leather shoes. He looked like a perfect musical-comedy Frenchman.

'You are an agent of the French government,' Holmes said rather stiffly.

'At the moment that is so, but I am like yourself a private detective. It is truly an honour to meet the greatest detective in Britain.'

Holmes rarely smiled but he did so then, although his smile vanished at the little man's next words.

'I am myself the greatest detective in Europe. My name is—'

The narrative ends here, so that the pseudo-chef's identity remains uncertain. The scandal of Sir Charles's death was evidently hushed up. Hans Mulready had in later life a successful stage career as a female impersonator.

Holocaust at
Mayhem Parva

A fine summer morning in Mayhem Parva. Through the leaded light windows of her cottage in the High Street Mrs White, who thought of herself as the merry widow, watched Professor Plum walking along erratically as always, taking care to dodge the cracks in the pavement. He looked deplorably untidy in that old pullover, but still she thought he was a fine figure of a man, and one said to be susceptible to feminine charm. If she was at his table at the vicarage tea party that afternoon, and sparkled – and she knew how to sparkle, who better? – anything might follow. A supper tête-à-tête, a little gentle dalliance, and then – well, she had really exhausted the pleasures of being a merry widow, and although the Professor had the reputation of being a permanent bachelor, interested only in the odd concoctions he brewed up in his laboratory, he had never seen the merry widow really sparkling. But of course it was necessary to arrange that she *should* sit at the same table. She picked up the telephone.

Outside Mr Bunn the baker's, the Professor had to sidestep dexterously to miss a couple of tricky hairline cracks in the pavement. An ancient Morris pulled up behind him with a shriek of brakes, the window was wound down, and the

Reverend Green's round shining countenance looked out at him.

'Is it not a beautiful day, Professor? All the live murmur of a summer's day, as the poet puts it. And where can the summer day murmur more seductively than here in Mayhem Parva?'

'Ha,' said the Professor.

'We look forward so much to seeing you this afternoon.' At that Professor Plum merely nodded. The Reverend Green put his head on one side and said coyly, 'A certain temptress has asked my dear Emerald if she may share your table.'

'Ha,' the Professor repeated.

'That makes you curious, I'm sure.' In fact the Professor had shown no sign of curiosity. 'I fear you must wait for curiosity to be satisfied. What I can promise is that Emerald has prepared a sumptuous spread. But I have duties, I must fly.' The ancient Morris moved off in a series of jerks.

The infernal Mrs White, I suppose, the Professor thought. Stupid simpering woman, not a patch on that fine little filly Mrs Peacock, what's her name, Paula. Now if it had been Paula Peacock who'd asked to sit at his table – but that wasn't likely, and it wasn't the problem, which was what to do about the Vicar. Should he go to the boy's parents, or confront the Vicar face to face and tell him he was a disgrace to the cloth? But suppose the man just laughed at him, and the boy's people sent him off with a flea in his ear? Difficult, difficult. Better have a word with the Wise Woman, he thought, which was his name for Miss Harple.

Back in his ugly little house near the station the Professor retired to his lab. He was working at the moment on a mixture made from spotted hemlock, which he believed to be good for asthma. Multiplex Chemicals had shown interest in taking it up on a commercial basis. But the problem of the Vicar was on his mind, he found it hard to concentrate and after half an hour gave up. He telephoned Miss Harple and asked if she could come over, as there was a confidential matter he couldn't discuss on the telephone.

'A garden is a lovesome thing, God wot,' the Reverend Green said as he leaned over the fence that separated the untidy vicarage garden from Miss Harple's neat rose beds, primrose and polyanthus borders, and rock garden cleverly devised in stripes of red, white and blue. Miss Harple, who was weeding the rock garden, straightened up but did not reply. Even in gardening clothes she looked elegant, her beautiful white hair perfectly dressed, her china-blue eyes innocent, or as some said icy.

'What does the philosopher tell us? That God Almighty first planted a garden, and that it is the purest of human pleasures.'

'But it was entered by the serpent,' Miss Harple said.

'Ah, you are too clever for me.' She did not deny it. 'Dear lady, may I venture to remind you that Emerald and I look forward to seeing you this afternoon in our rambling wilderness.'

'I have a guest coming down from London.' She elaborated. 'A gentleman.'

'Of course he will be welcome, the more so because he comes as the escort of our dear Miss Harple, solver of all our mysteries, elucidator of every puzzle.'

The Reverend Green passed a handkerchief over his face, smiled, bowed, opened his garden gate. Miss Harple looked after him for a moment, finished her weeding, went into the kitchen. She had much to do before her guest arrived.

The letter plopped on to the mat. Mrs Peacock, eating her single slice of dry toast, drinking her sugarless tea – she

171

knew the importance of preserving her figure – heard it, and shivered a little. When she saw the square envelope with its carefully printed capitals she had to force herself to open it. She read:

I KNOW WHAT YOU WERE DOING
WITH PROFESSOR PLUM IN THE
CONSERVATORY. GET OUT OF
MAYHEM PARVA YOU FILTHY
WHORE.

She put the letter beside the two others, deliberated during a long hot bath, and then went round to see Miss Harple. Mrs Peacock had come only recently to the village, and almost the first person she met was Miss Harple. They had met before, when Miss Harple solved the mystery of the missing Egyptian diplomat, at a time when Mrs Peacock was the Egyptian's mistress and was known as TouTou the Peacock Fan Dancer. Her maiden name, which in fact she had never changed, was Betty Sludge, but not unnaturally she preferred Paula Peacock and, as she told Miss Harple, wanted only to live quietly in Mayhem Parva, her days as TouTou forgotten.

Miss Harple read the letters, and then looked at Mrs Peacock with those blue eyes that, as TouTou had said when being questioned by her during the Egyptian diplomat affair, could see through a brick wall.

'Is there any truth in these stories?'

'None at all.' She giggled, then stopped as she saw Miss Harple's frown. 'Though Professor Plum is an attractive man.'

'But you were not with him in the conservatory – or the library as another letter says – or his study?' A shaken head. 'And you have met nobody else in the village who knew you in the past?' Head shaken again. The china-blue eyes looked hard at her. 'Of course if you left Mayhem Parva and returned to London—'

A third head shake, and the most decisive. 'I've bought my house. And I love it here. It's so peaceful, so *English*.'

'Very well. Leave the letters with me. I will think about them. And don't worry. Every problem has a solution.'

With TouTou gone Miss Harple returned to her kitchen preparations, but not for long. This time when the doorbell rang it was Miss Scarlett, who lived only a few yards away, in a lane leading off the High Street. Miss Harple did not care for Miss Scarlett, whom she regarded as a malicious gossip, but she could be kind and gentle in the presence of distress, and she saw that Miss Scarlett was upset. She sat her down now in the little sitting room crowded with knick-knacks, and asked what was the trouble.

'I have had such a shock. This morning, earlier, I was in Payne's the chemist, I went in to get some indigestion tablets, but also because — I wonder if you have heard the story about Elfrieda Payne and the grocer's boy, it seemed to me that he, I mean Mr Payne, was looking very *tense*, and when Elfrieda came down the stairs—'

'Miss Scarlett, I do not want to know about Mrs Payne and the grocer's boy. Something has upset you. You were going to tell me about it.'

'Yes, my tongue runs away with me. I got my tablets, turned round to go out, and came face to face with Colonel Mustard.'

'The man who has taken a short lease on old Mrs Cunningham's house now she's gone to live in Malta. I have met him once or twice, he seems pleasant enough.'

'Oh yes, he *seems* pleasant. But his name is not Colonel Mustard, and he is a swindler. He called himself Commander Salt when I knew him, and persuaded me to invest in his company. It was called Electric Car Electrics, they were going to make very cheap electricity out of old newspapers soaked in sea water, which would run a new electric car. He said I should make a fortune, but he disappeared and I never saw a penny of my money back. Oh, it was such a shock.'

If Miss Harple thought that a fool and her money are soon parted, she did not say so. She gave Miss Scarlett a cup of tea and one of her home-made scones, found out by a few adroit questions that it was unlikely Miss Scarlett would have a case for legal action against Colonel Mustard, spoke soothing words, and said she would speak to the Colonel. She reflected that there were several fools with money in Mayhem Parva, but she did not say that to Miss Scarlett.

Colonel Mustard, alias Commander Salt, alias Group Captain Fairweather, did his usual hundred morning press-ups, ran round the garden half a dozen times, ate a hearty breakfast which he cooked himself, said 'Top of the morning to you' to Mrs Middleton the cleaner, and retired to his study to look through the draft prospectus for Uniworld Military Disposals, a company which according to the prospectus was being formed to buy out-of-date military equipment in European countries cheap, and sell it to the Third World. As the Colonel read through the draft he talked to himself.

'Agents all over Europe – old uniforms, cooking equipment, armoured cars, all sorts of electrical gear, out-of-date planes – going for a song, my dear sir, going for a song – no question of military use, m'dear madame, planes converted for commercial use, armoured cars turned into jeeps, uniforms retailored as dungarees – endless possibilities – you'll see thirty per cent a year on your money – and helping people who need it, shouldn't consider taking it on otherwise.'

The Colonel made a few amendments, stood up, looked at himself in the glass, admired the soldierly look, the erect stance, the clipped moustache. 'Ready to go, m'boy,' he said. 'If I'm not much mistaken, there's rich pickings in Mayhem Parva.'

But Colonel Mustard was mistaken.

Miss Harple met her visitor, whom we will call simply the Author, at Mayhem Parva station, which had no waiting room and was hardly more than a halt. He was an awkward shambling figure, who was writing a book about Agatha Christie. Miss Harple had known her well, and had an encyclopaedic knowledge of the works. As they walked back through the village she told the Author of her busy morning, the Vicar's call, Mrs Peacock's visit followed by that of Miss Scarlett, her own call on Professor Plum, whom she had found messing about in his laboratory. The Author listened, enthused about the well-preserved village street, and was suitably impressed by Miss Harple's little Georgian home Mayhem House, the Waterford glass on the shelves and the bits of Minton china in cabinets.

'It will be rather a scrap lunch, I'm afraid,' Miss Harple said when they were sipping dry sherry. 'My maid of all work Marilyn is in bed with a gastric upset, and I must apologize for the place looking so untidy.' In reality it could hardly have been neater. 'And that means, I'm afraid, I shall have to give the Vicar's wife, Emerald Green, a hand this afternoon. There's a tea party at the Vicarage, and Marilyn was going to help with cutting bread, making sandwiches, all that sort of thing. If you'd like to come Emerald would be very pleased, but perhaps you'd be bored by a Vicarage tea party.'

On the contrary, the Author said, it would be a new and no doubt exciting experience. He wandered round the garden while Miss Harple laid lunch, noting the abundance of roses without a trace of blackspot or mildew, the pretty yellow jasmine climbing up the wall, the weedless grass, the

yew tree that separated this tidy garden from the overgrown
one next door. After lunch his hostess talked about Agatha
Christie, her shyness, her love of true English villages like
Mayhem Parva, her endless curiosity about tiny details most
people overlooked or didn't notice, her relaxed charm with
friends. The Author listened and made notes.

When lunch was over, and they had drunk coffee in a
shady part of the garden, Miss Harple went to lend a hand
at the Vicarage, leaving the Author to look round the village
before putting in an appearance at the tea party. He admired
the old-fashioned coloured bottles in the chemist's window,
and the sign outside the butcher's that said, 'Butcher and
Grazier, Home-Killed Pork', went into the well-kept
church, was amused by the name of the pub which was
called the 'Falling Down Man', went into one of the
flourishing antique shops and considered buying a Victorian
mother-of-pearl card case, but decided it was too expensive.
Then he made his way back to the vicarage, where the tea
party was in full swing.

There were little tables with four or six people sitting at
them, plates of sandwiches, scones and little cakes, dishes
of trifle, ice-cream. His hand was pressed by one that
seemed damp with oil rather than water.

'You must be the friend of our dear Miss Harple. *So*
good of you to come. Now let me see, where can we find
room for . . . ah, but here is the lady herself. Thank you,
my dear, I must confess to being a trifle parched.' The
Reverend Green accepted gratefully the cup of tea handed
him, and wandered away.

'Here you are, then,' Miss Harple said a little sharply.
'Do you like trifle?'

'Well – I think perhaps – not after such an excellent
lunch.'

'You'll find chairs in the corner, and there's a place over
here.' She led the way to a table where three people sat,

and introduced him. 'This is Mrs Peacock – Mrs White – Professor Plum. And here is Emerald with a cup of tea.'

Little Mrs Green said it was nice to see any friend of Miss Harple, and recommended the tuna paste sandwiches which she had made herself. The Author considered his companions. Mrs Peacock sipped her tea delicately, Professor Plum drank his noisily while eating a piece of fruit cake, Mrs White was occupied with a plate of creamy trifle decorated with hundreds and thousands. Mrs White spoke to the Professor.

'This is really delicious, Professor, do try some.'

'Don't fancy it.' The Professor made a harrumphing noise, and said to Mrs Peacock, 'Settling down all right, are you? All very neighbourly here in the village, that garden fence of yours could do with a bit of attention. Quite a handyman myself, if you need one.'

Mrs Peacock murmured that he was very kind, in a voice that sounded extremely refined. Mrs White tittered slightly, leaned forward, and said, 'I hear your laboratory is quite fascinating, Professor, that you make all sorts of wonderful old medicines there. I believe myself that the old remedies are much the best—'

She was interrupted by a prolonged high-pitched scream. There was a crash, a sound of breaking crockery. Mrs White stopped speaking to the Professor and said, in quite a different voice, 'Whatever's the matter with Colonel Mustard?'

The Author turned, and saw that a tall red-faced man wearing a blue brass-buttoned blazer was on the ground, writhing and crying out unintelligible words. He had pulled over the table as he fell, and lay in a welter of spilled tea cakes and sandwiches. The Reverend Green, Emerald, Miss Harple and a man wearing spectacles were beside him. The woman who had screamed put a hand to her thin chest and cried: 'I had nothing to do with it, it was nothing I said to him.' Miss Harple took her arm, and said, 'He's been taken ill, Miss Scarlett, nobody's blaming you. Doctor Playden will be able to help.'

The man with spectacles looked up from beside the body, and shook his head. 'I'm afraid not. This man is dead.'

Some time later the Author sat on a sofa in Mayhem House, listening while Doctor Playden and Chief Inspector Haddock discussed the case with Miss Harple. He was amused by the way in which both men deferred to her.

'You're sure you feel up to the mark?' the doctor said. 'I know you've been sleeping badly.'

'I am perfectly well now,' Miss Harple said, with her agreeable touch of acidity.

The Chief Inspector coughed. 'Up to a point it's straightforward enough. There was cyanide in his tea, the question is who put it there. The only other person permanently at his table was Miss Scarlett, though the Reverend Green sat there in between getting up to say hello to people as they arrived, and chatting with them.'

'And I believe three cups of tea were taken to the table by Emerald, Mrs Green.' The policeman nodded. 'And she just put them down on the table? So it was by pure chance that the cup with cyanide in it came to Colonel Mustard.' Miss Harple paused. 'Unless Mrs Green was the poisoner.'

Doctor Playden protested. 'You surely can't believe that.'

Miss Harple spoke gently, her blue eyes innocent. 'I am simply pointing out the possibility.'

The policeman and the doctor were drinking whisky, the Author and Miss Harple her home-brewed mead. She spoke again, slowly. 'Miss Scarlett had reason to dislike

Colonel Mustard, but I don't think any cause to wish him dead. I think in the circumstances I should tell you about it.' She did, and then went on: 'But I have a feeling—'

'Yes?' the Chief Inspector said eagerly.

'That perhaps this is only the beginning. There was an old farmer we used to visit when I was a child, and he could always tell the weather after there'd been a storm. The sky might be blue again, not a cloud in sight, but he'd say: "This was only the beginning, the real storm's still to come." I feel like that old farmer. The real storm's still to come.'

Miss Harple, as so often, was right. The Author, curious to follow the case and anxious to talk with her again about Agatha Christie, spent the night in the 'Falling Down Man', and at breakfast heard the news from the distraught landlord.

'Reverend Green's dead, sir, and that's not all. Ambulances been in and out the village all night, taking 'em to hospital. Doctor's not had a wink of sleep. There be so many taken ill, sir, it's an epidemic like except it's not. They say the Reverend died in his sleep, and I hear tell he was poisoned, they say it was all that tea party at the vicarage.'

The Author spent the next two days talking to people in the village. He paid a couple of calls on Miss Harple but there always seemed to be a policeman in discussion with her, either a sergeant with the autopsy reports, a harassed-looking chief inspector, or the chief constable himself. She was obviously too busy to talk about Agatha Christie, and seemed disinclined to discuss the case, or cases, with him. The Author paid a visit to Professor Plum's house in the company of Doctor Playden, and saw the laboratory. The doctor, indeed, was friendly enough to tell him the detailed results of the autopsies on the six victims. It was after he had learned these that the Author paid Miss Harple another, and as it proved his last, visit.

It was late evening, and his welcome was friendly, although not overwhelmingly so. Miss Harple was wearing a blue brocade dress, with a little lace round the neck and a matching piece of lace on her white hair. She looked elegant, but also frail and tired. She apologized for her failure to look out papers she had mentioned about Mrs Christie, but said she would send them on to him.

'I didn't come to talk about Agatha Christie. I came to talk about the case.'

'The case is solved. Mr Haddock agreed with me that there was only one possible culprit, Professor Plum.'

'But Professor Plum is dead.'

'Precisely. He had always been eccentric, and it is plain that the eccentricity turned to madness. He had the means of making poisons in his laboratory, and had actually produced some of those used. What he did was the work of a madman, and when it was done he felt remorse. Why are you shaking your head?'

'I think there is a different explanation. Would you like to hear it?'

'It has been a long day. Will the explanation take long?'

'A few minutes.'

'Talking is thirsty work. I know you enjoy a glass of mead. And perhaps you would like a biscuit.'

The Author watched as she filled two glasses from a decanter, and placed one beside each of their chairs. When she left the room to fetch the biscuits he changed the glasses. On her return he began to talk, aware of his similarity to a detective in an Agatha Christie story gathering the suspects together to explain the case. Here, however, he had an audience of one.

180

'There were six victims. Colonel Mustard, who died at the tea party, Miss Peacock, the Reverend Green and Professor Plum, who died during the evening or early night, Miss Scarlett who died in her sleep, and Mrs White who died early on the following morning. Each died of a different poison. Colonel Mustard drank tea laced with cyanide, Mrs Peacock an infusion of hemlock, the Reverend Green was poisoned by taxine and Professor Plum by gelsemium. Miss Scarlett took an overdose of chloral hydrate, and Mrs White was poisoned by arsenic.'

'She was an exceptionally tiresome woman.'

'It's interesting that you should say that. She was the only one to suffer a prolonged period of pain before death.' Miss Harple looked at him sharply, then sipped her mead. The Author drank a mouthful of his.

'It would seem at first glance that the killer was somebody with a passion to try out the effects of different poisons, chosen at random. Nothing at all appeared to link them. But that was not the case.'

The Author waited as if for questions, but Miss Harple did not speak.

'The link was Agatha Christie. All of these poisons were used in her stories. Cyanide of course quite often, most notably in *Sparkling Cyanide*. Coniine, which is derived from spotted hemlock, was used in *Five Little Pigs*, taxine in *A Pocket Full of Rye*, gelsemium in *The Big Four*. One of the victims in *Ten Little Niggers* took an overdose of chloral hydrate, and arsenic was used in a story called "The Tuesday Night Club". The murderer, then, was somebody with an expert knowledge of the Christie canon, something that ruled out Professor Plum, who hardly had a work of fiction in his house.'

'But he made coniine in his laboratory.'

'Quite true. Doctor Playden told me he was in hopes of it being adopted as a remedy for asthma. You were friendly

181

with him, often visited the laboratory. I think you took a phial with you on one visit, and filled it from his jar of coniine.'

'And where do you suggest I found those other exotic poisons?'

'Two of them from your garden. Gelsemium is derived from yellow jasmine, which grows plentifully up your house wall, and taxine comes from the berry of the yew tree. I noticed a fine specimen at the bottom of the garden. Cyanide is still an old-fashioned way of getting rid of wasps and arsenic of rats, although of course they have to be extracted with some care.'

'Chloral hydrate is not easily obtainable.'

'Doctor Playden prescribed it for you because you told him you were sleeping badly. You saved it up, and then with your usual thoughtfulness gave it to Miss Scarlett as a sleeping draught. I remember that after our discussion when Colonel Mustard died, you said you were worried about Miss Scarlett, and went to see her.'

Miss Harple straightened the lace round her neck. 'And I suppose you think I gave little Marilyn something to upset her stomach, so that I replaced her as Emerald's assistant at the tea party?' The Author nodded. 'You are really very ingenious. Ingenious but ridiculous. Nobody will believe this nonsense. Have a biscuit.'

He shook his head. 'When I tell the chief inspector about the yellow jasmine and the yew tree I think he'll take notice.'

'You really suggest I put those various poisons into the teacups?'

'Yes. You carried round most of the cups and some of the cakes. It wouldn't have been difficult to give them to the right people.'

'Arsenic in tea would taste distinctly bitter.'

'Of course. I should have mentioned that. You knew Mrs White liked trifle, and copied the Christie story in

182

which the arsenic was in the hundreds and thousands on top of the trifle.'

'There is one thing you have forgotten.'

'I don't think so.'

'The three teacups were taken to Colonel Mustard's table by Emerald Green, not by me. I couldn't possibly have known he would take the cup containing the cyanide.'

'Oh, that was clever. But then of course you took that from Agatha Christie too, and adapted it for your own purposes. There is a story in which the poisoner wants a victim and doesn't care who it is, anyone in a group will do. And you didn't mind which of the three at their table took the cup with cyanide, because all of them were going to die. The other cups contained the hemlock and the taxine.' He yawned. He felt very tired.

'I congratulate you. You were perfectly right.'

'Thank you.'

'You may have been puzzled by my motives. I simply wanted to preserve the reputation of this unspoiled English village.' Miss Harple leaned forward and looked at him intently. The Author found it hard to meet the gaze of those icy blue eyes. 'Colonel Mustard had plans for inducing some of our credulous residents to invest in his companies, and they would have been ruined. Mrs Peacock had a past which – I won't dwell on it, but she was really not the kind of person we want here. I did my best to get her to leave by sending some letters suggesting she was carrying on an entirely fictitious affair with Professor Plum, and telling her she would be happier back in London, but she insisted on staying here. A pity – I rather liked her. Miss Scarlett I did *not* like. She was a busybody, mischief-maker, tale-teller, really no loss. Neither was Mrs White, who always thought of herself as the merry widow, which meant that she set her cap at any eligible man she met, in a way I found most distasteful. The Reverend Green's conduct was scandalous – I shall say no more than that. And Percy Plum' – her voice, which had been jarring as a clatter of steel needles, softened to little more than a whisper – 'was part crazy, but part a wonderfully clever scientist. I was very fond of Percy.'

'Then why—?'

'Because of his discovery.' Miss Harple looked down at the carpet, her manner almost coy. 'In his experiments Percy had stumbled by chance on what crime writers have feared might exist for years, the undetectable poison. He told me the secret, and of course it is safe with me, but the silly fellow insisted it should be made public. Can you imagine the result for books like Mrs Christie's? It would no longer be possible to write them. Why didn't I use the poison, you may ask? That wouldn't have been fair play, would it? And when we try to imitate crime writers we must always observe fair play.' She broke off. 'You worked things out very well, but you made one mistake. Shall I tell you what it was?'

The Author nodded. He found it hard to keep his eyes open.

'You failed to notice that when I left this room to get the biscuits I could see what you were doing in the looking glass placed just over there, beside the bust of Agatha Christie. I had expected you to take the precaution of changing the glasses, and had prepared my own glass of mead accordingly. Of course, if you had not changed the glasses I should have knocked over my own by accident.'

'You mean—' The Author tried to rise, but found that his legs refused to obey him. He saw Miss Harple now as through a mist.

' "To cease upon the midnight with no pain" – a beautiful line, I always think. It is a minute to midnight now, and I think I can trust you with the secret of the undetectable poison. The three elements are . . .'

Those were the last words the Author heard.